Shocking

Encounters

With

Ben Bergman

Disclaimer

This is a work of fiction, any semblance to real people is purely coincidental.

New York | Boston | Paris

ISBN 979-8-9930962-0-9

October 15, 2025

For Meghan

Acknowledgement

For my children and my family, I will regret the time that I missed while writing. Thank you for the love and support.

For my patients and those suffering from a disease, know that you are seen and not forgotten by physicians, nurses, and healthcare practitioners everywhere.

To *Andy, Kate,* and *Dad,* I miss you like crazy. Hopefully, on a quiet day up there, if you listen hard enough, you can hear me making the world's most annoying sound to the kids.

Table of Contents

CHAPTER 1

A Letter Arrives

A few thin slices of eighteen-pound lay folded inside an envelope in the mailbox. Thin, so thin you could see right through it if you held it at eye's height, the thickness of knives, he thought. It would hardly affect him. It was brutal, but he would shrug this off just like everything else. He could tell it was from her, but decided to keep his options open for the time being and vaguely ignored it for a short while. It was nothing, a flattened piece of bark. A branch fell on the street in front of him the other day and had the same qualities as this letter, wood and bark and dryness and nothing else. He had not let the twigs enter his consciousness, brood there, plot and ponder, invade, destroy, infest—why would the letter?

He took a walk to break this incantation, this literary voodoo. He was not quite feeling right, at odds with the swaying trees, perennials, winter storms, a lizard seeking the sun, and volcanoes, how they erupt every so often. He had no rhythm. He felt that wherever he went, he could not escape it. He could barely take a step without feeling like he would fall right over. It was Fall. The wind remained full, pushed stiffly on his face and chest, and not a gentle breeze but a malicious wind, conjuring the strength of nature against all, degrading the significance of man and spotlighting his frail dependence on luck. Every SunShot angle in the city unmasked a chapped face, a grimy set of teeth, or taut biceps. So many in the city cherished the winter's approach: greenish gray skies, rotting park pastures, the ever-slippery windy hill where red-blotched greedy faces stared from above. Not him. Far from it.

Then he got home. The same bland stale box for the last few years. It was an apartment listing posted by three roommates who needed a fourth, a short newspaper ad paid for by the management agent, which he found out later was written by Anthony Parmenti's grandmother. Tony was the owner of a pizza joint around the corner. Their pizza was lousy. He ate it quite often for lack of better things to eat and because he had to say hello to at least someone; the Mexican dough-spinner there was more amiable than most. Tony's grandmother was kind and probably the only honest soul Kyle had dealt with in years. She died soon after. From there on, things went south, the hallways unswept, the locks broken. The delinquent heaters whined and spewed into pools of putrid rust.

The roommates were raucous to say the least. Mick, son of an athlete, found out after fifteen years of running, pole vaulting, biking, and climbing, that the only sport he truly enjoyed was pot-smoking. Brady was an aspiring alcoholic, news junkie, and actor. Jose was the most normal of the crew, a writer for The Wall Street Journal, married, his wife raising his child in Marlboro, New Jersey; he could not deal with the commute, so he spent his weeks in this cheap apartment, mostly writing and smoking cigarettes outside on the lanai, talking to his wife and child on the cell phone. Sometimes he spent the weekend in the city, and his wife brought his child into the city; they argued from time to time, but appeared happy.

The letter in the mail had started across the Atlantic. With it, he imagined, myriad others crowd surfed in a mail bag and sweaty with import all the way to the Upper East Side of New York. There, the wind blew swiftly, messing the hair of Kyle's downstairs neighbor, the Chinese restaurant owner who kept his own share of the greasy grey world what he considered clean with a broom and hose. His rosy cheeks and yellow teeth shone sharply against the pavement, floating in a dream of happy work. Mr. Lee—not his real name Blythe found out one day, speaking with him, Jie Zhang's was "too Chinese" for the average restaurant-going New Yorker—often ignored streetgoers when he watered down the sidewalk. Women in dresses, men in suits, he sprinkled their pant cuffs and doused the occasional freshly groomed poodle. Kyle liked him very much and never went to his restaurant.

Mr. Lee focused on his broom handle, and Kyle headed upstairs. He rubbed his eyes on the way upstairs—in the process dislodging mountains of soot, some would call it dirt although Blythe actually felt it was just an overly dry eye problem, not to mention that decades later the resolution on this problem— mind-numbingly simple—would bring to a head a long, protracted, poorly articulated mental/physical struggle inside of Blythe which most succinctly can be stated as minor health problems with easy and commonly available solutions but which he ignored, or failed to recognize, or did not have access to the part of one's intellect that can step aside and self-analyze to detect the absence of easy good living, and these would giving him suffering pains or just chronic background life-irritation—producing one gigantic globbery wet drop which fell slow motion onto the words "Paris, France" which adorned the letter around where its belt-buckle would be. Once in the house, it established a presence right away. It lay there curiously on the coffee table for a few days, balls of dust indolent below and rice embedded in its unsquared hinges; such marinades—a few ounces of chaos, some diced slothdom, a few pinches of pornography—took time.

He had much to attend to. The roommates—Mick, Jose, Brady, plus the dog — had made a mess, and he had to clean that up, or get them to clean it up. There were one or two overdue library books, and in his closet, the largest pile of laundry ever assembled in anything other than a hospital. His plant, one of seven he had killed in as many months, needed watering on a daily basis; this was an ongoing responsibility. Many other things, some smallish, some larger, would occupy his time over the next months, so he could forget about this silly little script.

He had always been such a regular person, no tics or oddities. There were no known psychiatric problems in the family. He had never even had an abnormal mole. No troubles with school or violating the law; it wasn't worth doing anything that made people pay so much attention. He was of average build and average weight, with normal intelligence. Clothes were not a problem for him; he had access to them, and they fit. Dark-blonde hair topped a slightly large head. Most people thought he was a good-looking man. He usually floated along just at the top of things.

But she had him just where she wanted, at least he thought so. To be in love, then to look askew at your love but for a moment, question it, deny its existence, scoff or dare laugh at it, glance at another woman or stick something unkind in your bag of deeds, sulk a day or two, these are the awful prescient reminders of lost love. Just by sight, a quick look at the script, then away, he could tell it would make him do something. He felt something press on his insides, a rekindled pain, which he had not felt for years. He tried to resist, to drive this feeling deeper into his gut where it would dissolve in the chaos of living things. But it persisted, like rain on a day you desire to go out, or a fever when you want to be well.

This little note did not have an aura of malevolence. Oh no, it bulged a bit, exuded a scent of deliverance, pressed in good feeling, and licked spit-shut to dirty hands. As with most things, the essential meaning of it was laden with temporality, the incompressible finity of existence penned through in just more than two dimensions, and from a certain viewpoint, each inked symbol a skyscraper of meaning—a nonsensical "o" without a cunning vowel to woo it into existence—what powerless idiots we would be without words.

She had probably known he was in a state of extreme arousal, yet drugged down to the deepest knell of urban illness. Signs of it were everywhere. He looked in some eyes and saw immediately their scams, their hands filled with the grease of lies. In others, the misdeeds were worn in symbol. Unguilty with flimsy shirts and slack arms slung on a pole, their teeth piercing lips freshly marked with hate. He hardly thought about prying it open. And yet he knew this could be what he had been hoping for all this time. He had waited so quietly, seduced specific paths of life and lied to women and cajoled his way into meals with repugnant men of power, proudly fended off all other circumstances; he had performed these menial tasks of self-preservation for years upon end, for if he was not alive, it would not come at all.

It hadn't always been like this, please be reassured. You may not like a tale with a miscreant or a loner straight out of the gates, not that we have a loner on our hands here, and you read on and on, hoping to find the earlier essence of some good person gone awry, only to discover the tale of a miscreant from birth. There's no excitement in that. No woman would fall for such a being, unless she was an abhorrent creature herself. There are such abhorrents alive in this world, believe me, not that the present we are about to describe fits into such a category, although admittedly, there will be times when, for dramatic reasons, she will be portrayed as such. Please be comforted that she is the most beautiful woman in the world, the touch of her hand more soothing than aloe vera or slippery elm, and she is sometimes kind.

There was no clear reason to have this feeling, or not to have it. No matter. There was no need to even clarify the feeling. It was what it was. It was the acquisition of materials, writing supplies, and transcription skills that really mattered at this time. What use was there for these transient messages, yelps, and texts that were void of lust? Out, spoken word, God of war! Kyle, he told himself, try not to warp your mind or gouge out your eyes as you read this: nothing in these words (or any words) will help you, not ever, unless you burn this paper to turn cold into heat or raw flesh into something digestible or substitute it for low-grade cheesecloth. He thought these words were smut, insane smut, not even the good stuff that turned a person on. It was harsh internal suffering laden with satanic verse, the stuff of the cancerous and aged, the thing witches and paganism were born of, the ire of the ages, senseless shit, the bane of the church's existence, the murder of young women and children, the filth of the streets, pure trash and really good fodder for nightmares, nothing you would prep for any test with, no sense in reading this on the beach or in some back alley while waiting for a friend, nor is it killing instructions or anything similar to mystery.

How could Kyle arrange affairs without the proper materials? Simple items: pens and a decently weighted telephone and a tablet of good paper, not legal, so that you felt you were suing yourself, but a few nice clean-smelling sheets of twenty-pound pound. Nothing more than twenty pounds is required. Not drawing paintings here. There is no need for ink absorption of Rorschach effects. Simple missives, that is all. Come here. Yes, or no. Whens and with whoms.

The only matter of importance was to hear her laughter. The sickly-sweet inside of an emotion. Hair, sweat, tears, red-faced, blustery hot. The pristine calm of waking. A warm, touchable hand and sunshine in the eye. Fatigue after struggling to comprehend each other. The grotesque sound of one another eating.

It felt like nostalgia, but he remembered nothing. A few flecks of cognition, nothing more. The closest approximation of a definition, if you so require, might be a vague sensation of absence without knowledge of what was missing. It was a city, sure, that much was true, and he was pretty damn sure he was a living Human Being, not the aberration of someone's sick dream or the invention of some lunatic. But sometimes he felt that a shade darkened his perception, relegated him to a colorless, dizzy amnesia in this place with no culture, no history, where no one meandered or wandered, no street conversations, no gatherings or societies, no street music or celebrations, none of that.

Anyways, she had left in quite a hurry. The final image of her...wait a minute, let's not quite go there quite yet. Finality and finity are such morose concepts. Let's focus on infinite things, like the universe, love, freedom, and beauty. How about morality? What sorts of things can occupy the mind better than these thoughts, these thoughts without edges? One could spend the rest of the time pondering only one of these concepts, and even if he or she had been relatively immune from direct experience with one of them, for sure, eventually one would be struck by the death of a loved one, or jealous thoughts, and would therefore be able to dissect his or her interactions with the concept. Whole lives are born from such ideas, are they not? Consider architects, engineers, painters, and actors, right from the beginning, searching for a single strong idea. One person might be inspired by a number such as Pi, another by the sun, or the appearance of crowds of people. One could spend an entire life studying or pursuing the making of money, and he would be either a banker or an economist, or a financier. Let's take this further: entire civilizations actually could be based on a single infinite idea. Take the concept of freedom, for example, or say liberty to make it more historical. Have you heard of the United States of America? It would fascinate many people to discover the central ideas of old civilizations. We probably think we know them, but I bet we are wrong. If we see New York City underwater in a million years, or any American town for that matter, will we think the central idea was money or freedom?

If we must: the final image of her is from behind a half-closed door and a fork falling from a box, quivering. It was the box quivering, really, not her, and inside it were her belongings mixed with some of the things Kyle used to think had been his. They were no longer. He refused to help her because at the time, he thought she was not serious about leaving. The box rustled in her arms as she readjusted. Plates and bottles clinked. Please note that it was the plates and bottles doing the clinking; her hands and lips, and hair were remarkably still. Actually, she looked straight out gorgeous that day. Forget it, she was damn hot. Her cheeks were red.

A fork fell. The fork hit the floor, and she winced, perhaps thinking of episodes in the past where she had disappointed her mother. There may still be a slight dent in the floor to this day.

Maybe I'll write you someday when I'm over these things, she said. That was the real kicker. It was conditional, and it seemed finite, at least the way she sold it. But there was that "maybe" which they hung on to. He hung on to. Maybe I'll kick you in the head or shoot arrows through your eyeballs or cut off your arms and legs. Maybe. The timing of the whole thing was totally fuzzy. For a few days or weeks, he even kept buying and chopping up food for two, then he would scrap the whole meal and go out for a long walk, only to come home and forget that he was going to be alone again.

She may have left a few years ago, or a few months ago; he wasn't sure. He was unintentionally inflicting a cast on himself, intentionally. To keep thinking this way was punishment he did not deserve. He tried to move around, sweat, overeat, and smoke, but none of these things helped. The expensive bricks, the bland banks of flowers on Park Avenue, the queer statues marking expensive apartment buildings, the parades and skylines, perfect alleyways, their desired effects were useless on him. Artists, what scum. Entire museums rendered useless in his eye, for he appreciated nothing and despised everything. Had every artist in existence simply substituted a sharp knife for a paintbrush and painted their internal carotid lovingly with a quick, deep stroke of self-hatred, then, maybe then, Kyle would applaud them.

It's true that she left in quite a hurry. At the time, her emotions had flowed, gushed rather in spurts of speech, only pausing for breaths and one sigh before she departed. She looked so content and well-hydrated. Included had been a flop of the hair and a unique gesture of the hand. But there was a trace of concern in her face, too. Many nights, Kyle has deluded himself that it was a hint of regret, a pinch of uncertainty. These things practically make him nauseous now to even think of them.

And yet it was the last beautiful thing Kyle had seen. Ever since that day, as he crossed the avenues, perhaps a dull sunset setting in at the cafés down the block, he found himself sighing often and heavily. He would ponder patterns in brick and tile bathroom walls with hands clenched in his pockets, his most faithful companion the odd drinker who, pissing on the wall, discussed his rambles with no one. Kyle listened in as if he were his therapist all along, the thoughts in his own head far darker than the most disturbed of his clients.

The Fall had exploded like a bomb of sadness, the street littered with a shrapnel of leaves, mittens, chicken bones, broken hearts. At times during his walk home—coming from nowhere—he was convinced trees would fall right over. One might land square on top of him, desultory. There would be no surprise. It would happen in slow motion and without pain. If the pavement were to cave in, crumble into soft sand, and welcome him, he just might take it. Underground, he would lie humbly and ponder his life's sequence of events and wait for the worms to watch him choke.

The final scene with her had been in the apartment hallway, from behind a fireproof steel door. She was outside the door. Already, Kyle thought. No discussion or bargaining. He was sure she was leaving altogether. There was no odor on her breath, but a waft of ammonia from down the hall. There was a dingy yellow light in the hallway, and as the elevator descended, it cast a brighter hue on the floor through the wire-laden window in the heavy door. He could not say whether she had yelled or whispered, or even screamed, for that matter. She could have written it in the form of an e.e cummings poem:

maybe

ill

> *write*

you.   some day

whenimoverthesethings,

And still the phrase would 'stick in his mind.

And then she was gone. Her footsteps went pitter-pat-pat-pat pat pat so very rapidly down the stairs to the next landing and then out of earshot. These footsteps lingered in his head, not a voice or a situation, just the pitter-patter. Sucking her breast was gone. Holding her hand was gone. Doing her dishes was gone. She was really gone, for she hadn't left a thing behind. Except for the dink of the fork. Well, maybe there was a hair or two on further looking, perhaps a piece of soap which had touched her skin. Her smell lingered on the bed sheets and pillowcases. It even got stronger, perhaps. But certainly none of her belongings lingered behind. She had even taken what minuscule amount was left of her rancid sesame oil. She had left completely.

At various times, she would return to him, of course. After a prolonged meal, a flash of her from afar. Then, sometimes bits and pieces of her body—an ear, an index finger, or a small toe, white teeth in a fraction of a smile—would appear and then vaporize in his mind, just as he came out of the shower, or when crossing the long avenues. No matter how hard he tried, he could not picture her face. Of course, every now and then, a waft of her shampoo on the street. He wanted the memory of situations, things she had accomplished, and her ensuing reaction, but there was nothing there. Certain things would come to him, though. Her mother, for example, had always impressed him. She was such a kind woman, eerily smart. She rattled off a list of songs and musicians one day that left Kyle reeling. They were songs her mother thought she'd like to hear at their wedding. She and Kyle had been quite serious as a couple. Her father was a mathematician. He kept to himself at times in the basement with a book of Shakespeare, sometimes Russian books, but not Tolstoy or Dostoevsky. He had even written a book about business in Russian.

Sometimes it was one of those brownstone entryways that brought her in, the warm stones red and gray and then cold. Restaurants they had been to, bars frequented, mindless conversations, parks they had strolled alongside, emotions unfinished. These thoughts had vanished to some unclassifiable part of his mind which collected their essences and banished them.

CHAPTER 2

Lola

It easily could have been Waikiki. Black leather boots, a red button-down shirt, and a short black skirt had raised the temperature in Lola's core to levels unsurpassed in recent hangover meltdowns. Nearly impaled by a surfboard-toting hipster getting on the subway, she sidestepped and dismounted the burly train. A brim of sweat nested on her lip as she stumbled from the subway up to a bodega on the sunlit street up above. A young, toothy Indian guy sold her a pack of cigarettes but was so dumbfounded by her looks that he forgot to give her change for the twenty, and just handed her back the twenty. He held a smile for the duration. Lola didn't even look at the change but stuffed it into a self-hemmed pocket inside her skirt, usually inhabited by a modest stash of hashish that, with its inguinal intra-undergarment location, would test the political limitations of even the most stringent shakedown.

It wasn't Waikiki. It was West 108th Street. The buildings here were five or six stories high, just low enough to let the sun angle onto the sidewalk at this late morning hour. Across the street, a woman with brown hair, whom she thought looked Russian, tended to green, flowerless plants. They were housed in low wooden buckets, maybe two feet high, with wooden flaps cinched by rusted iron bands – flowerpots they may be called. The woman barely had to bend over. She massaged the leaves and plucked rotten blooms.

Lola was a self-proclaimed filmmaker, despite the fact that she had never attempted to make a film. She decided that she would, though, soon after taking care of this liver thing she'd come down with a few months ago, and began seeing a surgeon, Dr. Pardon, for medical advice and large quantities of medicinal marijuana. In reality, he didn't prescribe it, though he said he would if he could, but he assented to Lola's request that he give her permission to buy it from reputable sources. She had said to him: "Imagine someone told you that you had to bear the most unimaginable human suffering...incurable human illness, liver failure, certain death...and told you further that you could no longer partake in any of the stress-relieving remedies that mankind has stumbled upon a.k.a. cigarettes and marijuana...imagine that and tell me I can't smoke pot anymore?" Dr. Pardon nodded readily and told her to go easy on it, but admitted that alleviating stress would be beneficial.

She took a few moments to watch the lady. Years back, she would have been jealous of her easy sex appeal, her fine, untroubled skin. Now she simply took a few deep breaths and felt that she was happier than ever with whatever time she had left. Maybe Dr. Pardon could hook her up with a few more years, maybe even a decade, as he had hinted.

She had just come in from overseas, Paris to be exact. This neighborhood reminded her of the banlieue surrounding Paris, the pervasive feeling of perceived oppression which flooded the area like a constant tsunami and drowned unfulfilled aspirations. The tragic part here was the perceived oppression. She was going to visit a few friends, almost brothers really, who lived on the fourth floor across the street from the bodega. She took one last look down the street, one direction the park, the other a Baptist church, now silent, and some folks sitting out on their porches in the warm autumn sunshine. Hints of a jazz band that practiced in the afternoon caught her ear, though so faint that she wasn't sure if it was an actual practice session or her own memory.

She climbed the four flights and made her way right through the door, always unlocked, which comforted her. At least some things stayed the same.

She entered the living room and kissed Mick, Jose, and Brady, the three roommates. They had recently taken on a fourth, someone she thought was lost, and she had found and introduced him to the roommates. It only took a few throw flicks of her hair to convince them to take him in, house him, and bring him up to their standards of filth. After the kissing and excitement and bragging stopped, she sat down, lit a joint, and started in on her day in New York. Kyle had been in his back, dank bedroom, but strolled out when he heard all the commotion.

"What a cool thing Harlem is," she said.

"Lola, how the fuck are you, babe?" Brady said.

Mick toned in: "Lola, you look amazing, sweetie." He sat back further in a leather recliner chair, happy to see his old friend. Of course, Lola protested being called sweetie.

She went off on Harlem and how impressed she was with its diversity. Her tight red shirt compressed her breasts as she leaned on her knees: "I called my friend. She agreed with me that it's like, wow, there you are, one moment you're not in Harlem, and then one moment you are. Lots of good eating and so forth. I saw a show about all the riots and devastation that took place during the blackout in the 1970s. What a fucking crazy fucked up night that must have been. It's a very cool place."

"Cool?" Blythe said, dejected. He had always had mixed feelings about his neighborhood. "What's so cool about this place? It's all either getting gentrified or getting so scared of gentrification that it's going backwards."

She unbuttoned her shirt one button to cool down and feel more relaxed. She blew smoke in Blythe's face, mainly addressing him now, through teeth the color of milky coffee. He had always thought that Europeans started drinking coffee at an early age. She looked like she started earlier than most.

Nonetheless, Blythe found himself drawn to her. He stood up, tired of the smoke treatment. He looped around the back of her, inspected her hair, her straight neckline, and her simple, perfect posture. It must have been simple motivation. She was a speaker, an electric one. Her words seemed to amplify themselves, echoing against the bored walls and chairs, and everything she said elicited a smile from almost everyone. Even as she sat there, limp hands across a subtle lap, the impression was profound.

Kyle hardly understood Lola. They had met seemingly at random one night after work at a shitty taco place he was earning some money at, and had a very brief exchange. Over the following weeks, it seemed like she was unavoidable, randomly showing up in the subway, at the coffee shop, in the strangest of downtown village bars he thought he was disappearing into to enjoy some true hard-fought loneliness. And there she was, always popping up in unexpected ways.

Of course, she blew smoke again in his face once he was in front of her again.

"Oh, you can't start to think like that. You need a girl, that's what it is. You can't resist the whole world changing. It's inevitable. Things will change whether you like it or not."

He smiled. His cheek twitched as the smile turned back down.

"You're probably right."

"Once you start having sex again, you won't think about it so much. You have too many smart, frustrated chemicals right now. Get in bed and get dull, you know?"

"There you go. Poor people can't have as much sex as wealthier people; they're too busy worrying. How am I gonna pay the rent, and is this job gonna make me miserably unable to afford my own goddamn neighborhood a few months from now?"

"Oh, there you go again. Go masturbate or something. What, you think capitalism makes people poor? Capitalism makes people rich. What's making people poor is laziness. I think you're quite wrong. Rich people are up all night pondering how to make more money. Poor people are having sex every moment they can or coming up with excuses to stay poor. It's the only thing they're motivated to do. Plus, the sex makes their feet hurt less during the long day, I will give them that, that it's cyclical. Tired leads to lazy leads to a lack of motivation. It's easier to stay poor than it is to make money, let's put it that way."

She paused and broke out a second joint.

"Look, it's all out there, unless you're lazy, anyone can make it rich, never mind a few obstacles such as racism, nepotism, you know."

She paused for a long time, and all were silent.

"Anyways, not everyone wants to be rich. They might talk about it, but if their motivation isn't there and they don't try, well, that's not really wanting something at all. That's just dreaming. That's like wanting to live in Polynesia when you hate having your ass full of fucking sand. When you're at the beach, sand is an all-consuming phenomenon. You can't avoid it. If you think you can, that's called dreaming. Shit. Speaking of beer, do you have something to drink?"

As Kyle laughed, Mick called her over to check out part of his script, something he had written. She blew one last puff of smoke in Kyle's face.

"We'll talk more," she said kindly.

Kyle grabbed a couple of Coronas from the fridge. Flashing bulbs that click and shut in the shape of the word Corona on a storefront imitate his intellect in falsetto, reminiscent of islands and cheap, weathered advertisements, scenes that resided nowhere except in the mind of an impetuous advertiser or a shiny boardroom placard. The constant acquisition and consumption made him feel totally alone in his body, his insides completely shut off from all else. He shut the refrigerator door and gazed past the Pizza Hut magnets for a moment, his mind dizzy. He thought that Lola was right in some ways, and wrong in others. He handed her a beer, and she took it without looking up from Mick's piece.

Kyle's filthy bare feet sloshed through water from the Xochi's dish. He was familiar with the feeling. A canine yawn caught his ear. The roommates talked hurriedly, as if their work was going to self-destruct if not soon, very soon, put into a less malleable form.

Lola, in the red shirt, told some stories about her experiences over the past few months in New York. Kyle wondered if she was loose with the truth, reporting times and events within a few details of the actual event, embellishing overheard conversations to make them more palatable, cataloguing her life in magnificent detail and hyperbolic meaning, all to sell herself, to heighten her image in the minds of those around her to the point of idolatry. Or was she naturally attractive? Was she actually magnificent?

He did not know, but wanted to find out. New to her name, he had heard the roommates talk about her. Much excitement about her coming to town. She must be something special, an abnormal person. There must be a way to find out the truth about her.

What had she experienced that made them all want to be with her—and Kyle did not deny that he already wanted more of her attention—to try to suck in her pleasures second-hand, to tour her mentality with our mouths agape at her every statement?

Lola, what had you done? What had you found?

CHAPTER 3

He had put himself into numerous positions all at once—artist, drunk, egalitarian, scientist, politician, waiter, astronomer, geologist, esoterician—to sift through all the possible permutations of his being, to weed out, filter-run himself through a purification, see which one would stick, in order to appeal to her sense of worth. But he sensed in all this commotion that the business he applied himself to may have obscured some central fact, a reason like gravity, an all-encompassing truth, a boiled-down belief of hers that was unshakable, that no matter what he did, who he was, or when he had done it, she always reserved the right to change her mind in a finicky twitch. It was so frustrating to have love that wasn't always love. She could realign the cosmos with a sip, suddenly tilt the verve towards unlikely places, organic farms, or undiscovered islands, or thoughts of whales' gullets. And all in a half second, half a frigging second, all his plans and machinations and years of caffeinaceous dreams were brought down like the child's best idea ever.

He wished he had a chore, a responsibility, a call to make, something to take away this grumbling stomach. He looked around the apartment for anything that might take his attention, stopped halfway into it because it made him feel even lonelier. Moving right on to a picturesque village, he envisioned themselves together for once, high on life, rearranging their priorities for a neatly planned escape from their routine success in high-power jobs while living on the edge of perfect fitness and happiness. They might jog six miles a day, rest one day on the weekends. A marathon was in the works for next fall. They had full sets of designer shirts and blouses with slightly intimidating collars, fashionable pant cuts, and esoteric collections of leather shoes guaranteed for life. They lived expansively with intense social lives in multiple cities across three continents. They thrived as the seasons ran by. In the end, they would die with gasps and wistful words at their graves from behind thin veils of black lace.

This was madness, and it was so terrible because none of this made him happy: not these thoughts, not the dinner, not the medications...but the letter. Now there was something about the fact that she had sent him a letter. He had put it aside a few days ago, out of fear.

There was some clue he had to wring from his present state of discomfort, faced with such impending decisions such as the one that lay not quite flat in front of him. So quickly things changed from the unattainable specks of thought which classified his life before the letter. A dull existence where intrigue, even action, seemed dreary, dramatic pursuits to drown the boredom. Now he was in a perfectly precarious state, balanced like a raindrop on the oncoming air. He felt that he could go out on the street right now, grab several high-class beautiful women, and sweet-talk them into dinner and hitting up a sophisticated music scene where they would grind in the back corner, her fur coat stolen at the end of the night, and lipstick and perfume on his expensive shirt. But that was the vodka talking, which he had imbibed a few moments ago to quell the nerves.

It was not an announcement, nor an invitation. He guessed by its girth and weight that it contained most likely some kind of bonded paper, two or perhaps even three sheets. It lacked the quality of a letter written in haste; this had been pondered over. Official notices or complaints did not come with the address handwritten, and certainly not in such an informal envelope which was obviously licked by a human, not a machine. She was not formal, anyway. She had never been one for ceremony or excessive public attention. He didn't particularly recognize the handwriting, though it very well could be a perturbation of her old pen, with a bit of sophisticated angst thrown in there like a spice. He ran his dry hand over the indented envelope and unsmudged writing.

Small and squarish, the envelope was not the type used for invitations or proclamations of marriage, and certainly not for business or solicitations. But he couldn't rule any of these out quite yet; she had gone this far, who knows to what sublime or subjugated level she may have inflated herself. It was a straight licker, not the festive "V" which might indicate celebration. Palpable wrinkles adorned the browned sheath, evidence of an active journey overseas. Hundreds or perhaps thousands of other dreams and perished loves had smothered it from every angle.

The envelope opened crisply; the sound may have even startled Blythe. He fondled the cheap French glue, yellowed and aromatically reminiscent of old cheese. What he had just torn open was a letter from France, and his hands shook slightly as he read the news that his ex-girlfriend would be in the city next week, along with her new British boyfriend, whom he instantly imagined to be a terrible person, although he admitted silently to himself that he wished to meet him. He grabbed his stomach, which now hurt.

She simply said "Matthew and I," which was frightening because it sounded so formal, so proper. She had never described the slouch, nor spoken directly about him, presumably out of decency, but maybe even explicit tactics to inspire jealousy.

She was capable of such things, capable of the kinds of actions that were only discovered by the passage of time, the resolution (or the non-resolution) of events, murky situations, with feelings whipped to a froth, pride, on the other hand, congealed into something stubbornly hard. He wasn't about to give in. But there was something about the name. "Matthew." She had written such an affectionate "M." Kyle wanted to tear him apart. He was probably a tax collector or something else ridiculous.

But then his feelings changed. It's a modern world they live in: facsimiles, electronic mail, hypertext, digitized voices, terabytes. Yet she had chosen to sharpen up an old gnarly pencil—a throwback to grade school, the taste of lead and chewed erasers—mark up a page with carbon, which in the end would signify, in Kyle's mind, some secret meaning. He imagined her turning her world upside down, racking her brain for inspiration and the will to commit to some want. Maybe she was unhappy with Matthew? Maybe she had desired that he would see thin and thick arcs, trailing scratches and unclosed loops, extraneous marks of passion, fits of compulsion, uncrossed zees, the generic beauty of her cursive, in sum, all the vagaries and idiosyncratic meanings of handwriting. He took this all to mean something very good. He filtered it with his own lens. Perhaps she had written automatic prose. Perhaps not. In his mind, each notch, crevice, and loop she had designed intentionally. Even if this was only his desperation, twisted, lonely thinking, even then, he was better off believing that she had intended to impart to him some message of urgency.

CHAPTER 4

It was 1976 when Lola first found out she had a disease. Well, actually, it was 1976 when her parents found out, but they didn't tell her. In fact, they never told her. She was too young and wouldn't have understood, so they thought. It would have been a great psychological burden, they felt. What they wouldn't admit to themselves, however, was the real reason: they didn't have the right diagnosis. She had abnormal liver tests, which were assumed to be benign. Her parents weren't really interested in advanced medicine, biopsies, that sort of thing. So they took the good old doctor's advice and kept a close eye on her. Sort of.

Her mother died young; one of the nurses said she had seen this before in parents of sick children. Her father committed suicide several years afterwards. Perhaps it was all the predictions and permutations the doctors had made—premature heart disease, kidney problems, destruction of her blood vessels by her body's own forces—all these terrible possibilities that ate away at their hope. Whatever the case, both of her parents were dead long before Lola was old enough to comprehend her condition.

Dr. Kenneth Pardon saw Lola on the first Monday of each month, save for December, when he went on his sole vacation of the year. Well, at least they had an appointment each month. Lola attended about annually over the last twenty-nine years, with more frequent blood tests in between the annual visits. The Doctor had never seen a woman so young and healthy deal so well with the idea of illness. Lola was not ill yet; she was barely even sick. Her liver enzymes were hardly elevated. Had it not been for Dr. Pardon, who took such a meticulous family history and uncovered a string of poorly defined liver disease coupled with psychiatric problems in the family, Lola probably would have died. It was a rare but known disease where copper was poorly handled by the body. But for sure, copper would accumulate in her blood, brain, liver, and kidneys, if she didn't eventually have the red organ "chopped out," as Lola liked to call it, and "a new one thrown in there," as she also liked to call it, she would die.

"Dr. Pardon, you realize it's very sexy, don't you?"

The Doctor looked her over, a hint of a smile on his face after her comment. He peeled back her eyelids, felt the sides of her face and neck in a solid grip, the hands warm and soft.

"What are you referring to, sweetie?"

"Being a doctor. I mean, the way you are a doctor. The..." She was cut off by Dr. Pardon lifting her shirt in the front to listen to her heart.

"I've got tiny tits, don't I?"

Dr. Pardon cleared his throat. He was used to this.

"How's it sound? Will I need a new heart, too, doc, from all this damn metal? Hey...doc, can I sell all this copper and make some mula? You know some of my old druggie friends steal copper pipes and copper plating sometimes to take to metal scrapyards to sell for drug money."

The Doctor was deep in the rhythm of the heart. His breath, now so close to Lola's face, comforted Lola with a trace of banana. He had a way of not answering certain questions, which Lola took as a sign of reassurance.

"What was that, sweetie?"

"Oh, nothing, I was just asking about my heart."

"The heart sounds fine, and it shouldn't be affected, as long as we transplant before you get sick."

"Dr. Pardon, what's the chance I'll die if I have surgery?"

"Lie back for me, Lola, so I can have a feel of your abdomen."

She lay back, slightly dizzy. The fluorescent light above took her to the operating room all of a sudden. As Dr. Pardon tickled her lower belly with an unafraid hand, she closed her eyes and saw him with a scalpel in hand, gowned in sterile blue. No nightmarish quality, actually, the opposite.

"There's no chance, Lola, I'm not going to let you die." Dr. Pardon said this matter-of-factly.

Lola noticed that Dr. Pardon raised one eyebrow more than the other when he was answering a serious question.

"Ever?"

He simply gave her an underwhelmed glance.

"No chance?"

"A very small chance. Let's put it this way. I haven't lost someone on the operating room table in...well...years, and I operate on hundreds of people a year."

"What's it like?"

He probed for her liver gently.

"Losing someone?"

Deeper now.

"Slicing someone open."

"Take a deep breath."

Slight crampy pain as he edged into the gallbladder.

"Okay, now let it out, Lola. Breathe normally."

"Okay, you can sit back up for me."

Dr. Pardon seemed overwhelmed for a moment.

"Slicing someone open," he said rhythmically, "as you call it, is one of the greatest experiences a man or woman can have." He sat down at his desk, the color of cypress leaves in summer, and instructed Lola to sit across. He'd once told Lola that Mrs. Pardon had recommended such a setup for patient counselling. She figured it was good to have some distance from the patient, to make boundaries clear.

"When you make an incision, Lola, your mind races and races to figure out how to get exactly back to that incision. The entire time in the body, whether one hour or twelve hours, my predominant thought is how to make this all better again. How am I going to close this incision? Every step along the way is geared towards closing, from tying tight knots to avoiding big blood vessels, to making a swift intervention with minimal exposure time. For you, Lola, it's going to be wonderful. When we are finished with your operation, you will have a one-hundred percent cure of your disease. It's not very often I can say that! We will have to deal with immunosuppression from then on, but that's not such a big problem anymore with the kinds of medicines we have...new medicines."

Lola sighed deeply. She took comfort, for some reason, in this rather technical description. She believed they would save her life. They would almost kill her, she was sure, by chopping out her liver, but in the end, it would be worth it. She had complete confidence in Dr. Pardon and his colleagues.

Dr. Pardon took a moment to write some notes, during which time Lola took a good look at him. He looked deteriorated from the years of hunched, early-morning hospital rounds, his cheeks ruddy and plump from zealous late dinners, and his ears chafed. His lips were pursed tight. Lola imagined this was from never having expressed either to his wife or his secretary, who were one in the same person, his unending love.

Now well-established as a surgeon, Dr. Pardon saw himself as an emissary for death and desire. To tease them, both of them, out of awful hiding was his job. He never approached quite close enough—sheltered by a chasm of hard brown wood—to get scorned by the hot fires he whispered into unwilling ears. To know a person was to see them at the news of their impending illness, hearty, or clenched shut. The hardest ones were the content, for on occasion, he wanted to die along with them; it seemed such a sweet repose.

Just then, Mrs. Pardon poked her head in the office door.

"I'm with a patient, can't you see?" Dr. Pardon beamed at her. He hated it when she interrupted.

"It's not just a patient, don't call Lola just any old patient. Mrs. Johnson is coming in tonight. Her hip is bothering her more this week. Don't you know it, she always does this to us on a Monday."

"Just the hip? Ah, listen, I'm with Lola, can you please let me finish with Lola?" he said, quite rudely.

"Hi, Lola sweetie. How are you feeling?"

"Doin' okay, thanks, Molly."

"She's short of breath too..." which trailed off as Mrs. Pardon exited.

The phone rang and Dr. Pardon rolled his eyes as he heard his wife answer and deter yet another patient from coming in so late on a weeknight.

He leaned back and put his hands behind his head.

"Lola, you look great. If it wasn't for your liver, I'd say go out there and tear them apart. You really look like you're doing good, no problems that I can find on your physical exam. All we have to do now is schedule a few routine tests prior to surgery. But the way things are looking right now, that will be a long time off. Believe it or not, you have to get a lot worse before we can get you better. We'll talk more about it next time. Come back next month. Think about timing. What kinds of things do you have coming up in the next few years? Your life will change a bit, Lola. You will be healthy and happy, but you will always be aware that you have to treat your body well. No more pot, no more smoking, minimal alcohol. Actually, I'd rather you smoked a small amount of marijuana and less alcohol. Just start thinking about it. What are you doing to keep yourself busy nowadays?"

"Oh, the usual, taking care of people."

"Still, that company you were telling me about? What was it, relocation assistance or something?"

Lola smiled in her mind. "Yeah, relocation assistance. Uh-huh. We help people move about in their lives."

"Alright, well, take good care of yourself, and we'll see you in a month or two."

He hugged her briefly and left.

While she felt happy to have seen Dr. Pardon, she felt very angry about the liver situation. What the fuck is cirrhosis anyway, and who the fuck decided to spell it with two r's, the same poetic motherfuckers who spell words like abhorred and diarrhea and catarrh and tichorrhine? But this was just the beginning of Lola's day. She had many things to do and many thoughts to think about. She had to figure out how to get her back, then figure out how to make her love again and how to make him capable of being loved he had developed this horrible smelly breath and beer gut, then figure out how to get her bar to make more money so she could do more, then finally when she was done with all that she could sit and dwell on this goddamn stupid fucking cirrhotic liver, hopefully before it was too late.

CHAPTER 5

Lola's Early Life

The family was a rusting fence. It was still there, but held nothing in and scared everybody away. Lola had sensed the family breaking up. She had for years. It explained a lot: the stressful car trips upstate, the crying spells certain family members would have at family functions, the silent phone calls she would not be allowed to overhear. Her aunt, far removed on a farm in northern Montana with four midget ponies as her only occupation, her grandparents dying slowly, the offspring split up like a diced onion all over the country, several uncles' dead now of lung cancer from heavy smoking, and multiple divorces, annulments, incarcerations, illegitimacies, and overall dysfunctional beings had drawn and quartered the family.

Lola had not found the courage yet to tell Kyle that they were related. Despite her years of searching for him, relegated to discover her past, to reconnect, to heal, to find her family and repair her wounds, she found Kyle six months ago and had been hanging out with him and his crew.

She did not know where she was raised from ages 4 to 10. She had vague recollections of Eastern seaboard beaches, Cape Cod felt right, but she couldn't place it, even after numerous trips and research. Some vague familiarity in some areas of the New Jersey shore, the Cape, and even DC. She knew she had been there, but couldn't place the names or faces of those she was with. It felt like a déjà vu. Incomplete memories, truncated and sad.

When she was ten years old, she was adopted by a California family, a teacher and a scientist, both mega hippies. They found Lola through a Koinonia adoption agency. Lola had been home-taught; she knew that much. She was well taught but had not been formally schooled. After adoption, she entered formalized testing, far ahead of her peers her age, and entered the fifth grade as the smartest and youngest kid in the class.

Her newfound parents were very kind and open with her. They were open to discussing her mental trauma from day one and were the kindest souls one could imagine to Lola. She was appreciative and respectful back to them, to the extent that a child could be.

They fed her emotional support; she fed them teenager angst, knowledge, and grit.

She recalled many years of therapy and had been on a first-name basis with her counselor for many years. She had no real dark baggage, but a lot of abandonment issues, and thoughts of sadness about the fact that, at least as far as she knew, her parents had given her up for adoption.

She did not know much of the story, nor did she really want to know. If giving a child up for adoption was justified somehow, she always thought there must have been a happier workaround. If there was no workaround desired, then she would rather not know the reasons. If it was something as banal as finances, stress, depression, or substance abuse, she did not want to know. If they did not love her, she did not want to know. She knew in her heart that she had been raised properly until age 4 or 5, she knew there had been love until then she could almost remember it, she had had no broken bones and she was well cared for until then, she knew in her heart that something serious had happened, either to her or to them, which made parenting either a fiscal or mental impossibility. There was nothing she could do about it, so she moved on. She had the most vague sense one could have of what her birth mother smelled like, and some flashes of memories, more vague and intermixed with imaginary memories and self-protection, she thinks as the years pass.

She went through phases of rejecting herself and her adoptive parents. She took a decidedly Bohemian path through life, one year wearing mostly pillowcase dresses when it was warm enough, with a hole cut out for the head. For five years, her back was always to the TV, even in a social setting. She did not partake in fast food and tried to minimize exposure to addictive products and additives. She smoked a shitload of marijuana in a responsible way.

These phases came and went over the years. Lola joined several non-profit enterprises, rapidly ascending the ranks, and raised money for housing charities and medical charities with ease. Her adoptive parents were extremely supportive, to say the least, of her endeavors. In many cases, they donated to her causes and helped her with publicity at the university and beyond.

She knew there were secrets in the family. The fix was not in the revelation. Some secrets were better left unsaid. She knew the only way to fix things was to rebuild. It would take effort, months or years of trying would go unnoticed, but maybe a flower would bloom here or there. Like a desert flooded, there would be growth; there had to be growth. She hoped things would begin if only she could figure out where to start. Things are often very hard to initiate. Nothing starts on its own, except for mold and flowers, but those have a history going back millions of years. If you want to start something, in general, the world is against you. Like a tide pushing back, wind in your face, falling down, failure, like the resistance of populations to change or reform, like

And then, like the break of dawn, it came to her.

CHAPTER 6

She made her way to Sasha's house, which was near Dr. Pardon's office. Sasha was home, two cans of paint deep into a huge canvas.

"Sash, I need your help."

"With what beautiful?"

Sasha was from Paris, but had spent a good deal of time living in New Guinea embedded with a small tribe as part of her doctorate of philosophy.

"Well, you see, I have this friend of mine, an acquaintance really, who it turns out is actually family, although he doesn't know it."

"OK, fine, no problem there. Awkward?"

"I didn't even know about him, about the fact that I even had a brother."

"He's your brother?"

"True. Let me finish."

« L'inconnu, comme c'est intéressant. »

"Well, let's just say it appears to me that he has got himself all fucked up, depressed as hell, malfunctioning, a real waste of life really."

"Is he a suangi? He sounds like he may be one."

"No...well, he may be. I mean no, for sure he's not."

"I'll kill him if he's a suangi. I'll do that for you."

"No, you can't kill him, he's my brother."

"Doesn't matter. One of my husbands was a suangi and I killed him."

"OK, chill, killer sister."

"I will kill him if he needs to be killed."

"Girl...if you kill him, I'll kill you."

"Oh my god. You just told me that if I killed him, I would become your suangi. You have just silenced me. OK. Je comprend. I will not kill him. Je ne le tuerai pas."

"Jesus, you are a deadly girl."

"So what do you want me to do? Are you sure I don't need to…"

She glared at her, then laughed.

"Ok, so what I need you to do is just to scare the hell out of him."

"Oh! So he is a suangi?"

"Damnit, he's not a fucking suangi whatever that is!"

"Alright, alright, so he's not a suangi. Are you sure?"

"Listen, he's messed up in the head, and he needs to be changed. That's all. Just frighten him, scare him, that's all. No killing."

"I tell you what. Tell me where he is located, and I will scare the suangi out of him. I do feel this man will become a suangi one day soon. I will scare him so he will not need to become suangi. You see, in all of my studies, I have realized that it does not truly matter if you are suangi or destined to become one. 'Tis the same thing. D'accord?"

"Yes. Oui. D'accord. Thank you, Sashy. You look hot today." And with that, she let out a screech laugh and kissed her on her forehead.

CHAPTER 7

A Well-Intentional Man

Winter was bearing down fast. You could smell it through the windows. For the third time since he had abandoned a small dinner, now cold, Blythe eyed his medications. He had seen a doctor, some scam artist from the phone book. It had not helped, probably made him worse. Dim yellow streetlight oozed through the windows. It shone sickly yellow on some magazines on the floor. A taxicab honked impatiently downstairs, and Kyle could barely make out the sound of people on the sidewalk, deadened by the cold wind. The room smelled like cigarette smoke, but the roommates had not been home. He shifted regularly in a hard chair near the window and waited for the remainder of the night to happen.

There was no prospect of anything happening. And yet he was kidding himself. He didn't want to do anything. He wanted to plan, take notes, enliven his soul, which had been…resting…for so long he couldn't believe it was happening again. He had grandiose images of romance, traveling, the sublime nature of food in foreign restaurants, and beautiful, clandestine cemeteries. But then, just a few seconds later, a dejected feeling. A heaviness settled back into the room.

He didn't even want to go anywhere. It had been such a tiresome season for Kyle, replete with upped dosages and refills, a prescriptional nightmare really. He dreaded the pharmacist's beady eyes and chapped hands, and after a profuse sweat would set in, he would even consider querying the chemist about metabolic disturbances, but often lost the desire to do so with a hand swipe across the forehead and a convincing thought that perspiration was a natural phenomenon. Sometimes he'd find his shaky lip on the verge of blurting out some unanswerable question about nervous conditions.

He found that after visiting the pharmacist, he had to spend a few hours in a diner or some quiet, sweet restaurant to calm himself. But it had not come all at once. It is really quite vague and indescribable. It was a negative symphony, a conspiracy by no one to form a swirling brew of nastiness. His grandfather was dying, along with him, powerful currents of veneration. His girlfriend had left him for a Parisian man. Food had become disagreeable, so had going to the movies. Rashes and sores were commonplace, with headaches taking the lead from time to time. Of course, some of this can be blamed on the city. In its own desultory way, it was wearing on Kyle.

As for the rest, there is little that can be conveyed through description. It must be felt, experienced, driven through from beginning to end, like a chemical whose concoction depends not only on the ingredients and proportions, but on temperature, order, and speed. Otherwise, lives cannot be understood— people stand next to each other all over the place, waiting in line or standing in awe, some happy, some pondering their own death, their suffering unsurpassed.

Their problems dissolve in the salve of the city, only to disappear into the endless sewer and resurge at times in pools of iridescent green. You might not know what we're really talking about here if you're a suburban type, if you feel breathless around poplar trees and picket fences, rather than burnt out eyes and gray faces and clothes worn thin as onion skin. You can peer into these city eyes, shine a light in their throats, or stick them with something sharp and take their blood—you will not be close to mentality, opinions, feelings. And it all seems equal, the suburban and the urban, the togetherness of families counteracted by money and murder.

For Blythe, the tenuous was commonplace. In fact, he stood up loudly from the chair and made his way to a bar. Shortly thereafter, he found himself far from everything, comfortably slumped on a barstool. He twiddled his fingers while waiting for a drink. Already, he was planning medication intervals, how and when he would take which pills in what order, and with what kind of liquid to best avoid the uncertainties of malabsorption.

The bar was a local dive. He settled in quite naturally as he had done many times before. His liver hung over his belt, under a cheap, smoke-burned bar. A long ember in his hand flicked a spark onto his leathery arm from time to time. The wince and smother was delayed by some immeasurable amount of time, which, after a moment, was a source of embarrassment for Blythe, since the average onlooker—not that there were any—may have confused this for a fit of freakishness, some syndrome, or perhaps a spasm. When an uncomfortable like Blythe frequents a dive, he strives for an outward appearance of goodness, a well-intentioned man out at night for a few alcoholic beverages after a hard week of work.

Deviations from this image, upon realization by the uncomfortable, multiply—a patternless fractal beyond the scope of control, and the evening digresses into the unknown. Thoughts prey in this area, thoughts so malicious, so empty really, it is the stuff that inspires confessions to strangers, long swoon-ridden nights, and breathless early morning encounters with yourself when you dwell on dark secrets, observe your weaknesses of flesh firsthand through squinted eyes.

Yet this perch was his only inspiration. From here, he watched lives unfold in front of him. Sometimes it made him feel better. Of course, the best part was that he could watch, and watch only. He didn't have to get his hands dirty in the nasty, blood-soaked affairs of others: other people's abuse, neglect, greed, ignorance, shame. He could stay clear of it yet absorb the vapors, analyze them through his foggy gaze, all the while lapping up his drink at the bar like a sick bird. Only rarely did his blood boil when a man grabbed a woman roughly, and at these times, he felt lucky to have little courage, for he probably would have slit several throats.

There are three women in Blythe's life: his mother, a woman he loves in Boulder, Colorado, 1543 miles away, and his roommate's dog Xochi. She, Xochi, preferred to sleep in Blythe's bed, for reasons unknown to its owner, although reasons had been postulated. Among the most popular was the smell of meat, ever since Blythe slept with a ham, egg, and cheese sandwich, mashed into his sheets by spastic fits. The woman he loves had slept in his bed as well. She hasn't eaten ham since she moved to France, only turkey. She was tirelessly suspicious of food contamination, which was one of her less endearing qualities.

Kyle was quite certain that Xochi loved him the most purely.

He took shallow breaths into sore, spongy lungs, seemed to wring them out with each exhalation. Later on, the spiteful stomach gurgled and chirped on the way home from the insidious bar it had despised for years. He had decided it was a good night to quit drinking early, get a step ahead of his heavy thoughts. For sure, the roommates would rise late in the morning and be riotous and hungry, at least he had that going for him.

For four years, Blythe had done this: a quick drink here and there after work, the flood of emotions which he quickly quelled with a wave of the palm or a shaky finger, hacked his way through the continual ember between his fingers, and felt jolly most of the night long. Of course, time has kinks in it. Nothing is fluid. Every now and then, the music would stop, the humiliation of a complaint far more painful than clinks in the jukebox. It felt like someone had committed a crime. It was nonsense. The wound gaped, oozed shame. The break in his pattern reminded him of irregularity, mistakes, the awful passage of time, and death essentially. He felt that his arm, resting on the sticky bar, might smell of rotting flesh. He steered clear of it, at the same time assured himself that the adjacent female patron wore no face of detection. There was no remedy around, not for thousands of miles. On these pathetic nights, he would exit abruptly and trudge on home past the desolate alleyway where he often considered a deposition of vomit.

Trips home from the pub—often we get sick of calling it a bar, such a crude name— were sometimes the worst. Blythe pondered the ordinary to drown out other thoughts. Walks and food and bathrooms, light-switches and tables and linoleum, each thought comfortably lost in his mind. He was headed home, after all, not to some indecipherable location. He was not looking up at street signs, not even a glance. He had no need to even check his location. No wondrous contemplation of directions of any sort, not here. No gazes or confounded turnarounds.

So lost in the act of doing nothing at all, he forgot for a few moments that he was in misery. In fact he loathed himself, his own image he caught in barroom mirrors, the dark forehead angles he would see in glitzy store windows towards which he pretended to cast a pejorative glance, the down-turned lip he carried above and below his rotting teeth which, except for a few engraved items like a watch and a money clip, are the only things he would welcome in his casket as means of identification.

There came in medication. In their countless forms—the creams and medicated alcohol rubs, jelly pastes and absinthian oils, camphoraceous balms, acid washes, ant piss concoctions, analgesics, stabilizers and tranquilizers, nullifiers and anti-depressants, inhibitors, inducers, antacids, salts, enzymatic emulsions, and other nonsense, and above all, for Kyle, the last resort, the cure of all cures, the medication of extraordinary potential: the picture of her with Colorado mountains in the background, her face far away yet distinguishable, set in an unburnable steel frame atop his musty dresser, neither of which had been moved in years—they were usually the only route left. Four years of acknowledged dust had accumulated on the tiny rub-worn ledge of the frame, a till upon the foothills of his imagination. Sometimes a cold draft would find its way through the glass, and he would feel quite sure that he could smell mountain air. Rest assured, it is quite intoxicating. Despite the deluge of procrastinated phlegm that warm weather would conjure from the depths of his lungs, not unrelated to the many times he had considered depositing the chest on the corner of a nameless street, smashing the picture, never mind that its placement in the category of refuse would send it straight to a suffering-locked chamber in his heart, something was about to give.

CHAPTER 8

A Blind Man

Lola had spent enough time in the apartment to pick apart the lives of the roommates on some superficial level of life criticism that operated something like: they watch TV too much, which probably is why they smoke pot, because they need the mental freedom from the regimented programming of television. She decided that they were overly basted with testosterone and pornography, although she was not opposed to either of these in moderation. She desired a bit of mental stimulation to counteract the forces of male slothdom. Either that, or she was stoned herself.

"Science without social input is nonsense," Lola commented to the roommates. Cognizant of a youthful dialectical tendency amongst these mood-altered consumers, Lola attempts to lure them into discussion with a seemingly well-thought-out aphorism.

"Scientists that are not watched over by the whole of society, or at least well-meaning disinterested observers, are the worst kind of tyrants. Think of a scientist like Einstein...someone who comes up with great theories in private...and it takes us so damn long to decode his thought process that before we figure it out, we've already accepted it and formed a world view. By the time we understand the logic and come to refute it, as we always do, we are too confused to change the way we live and too proud to accept the fact that we were stupid. We need explanations, convenient truths. And if not that, then at least conjectures, hypotheses, best guesses. But usually, we don't get past the theories, and we crave truth so badly that we settle for opinion and questionable knowledge. Thus, Einstein becomes a tyrant because we are unwilling to spend the time to learn his beauty, and we are forced to accept his explanations at face value. It takes years, decades, before we put them into interpretative discourse."

Lola was on a rampage against modern civilization and its presumptuous claims of enlightenment. In her opinion, admittedly unsubstantiated, unsubstantiated forms of thought are readily absorbed into culture by a process, not unlike a high-school Student Council election, in which the simplest, most confidently stated, most barbaric, and, in place of all these words, most "popular" idea gets accepted as the rapid truth. Interpretations and observations, made with eyes whose blind spots are just as susceptible to the mind's creativity as any other lunatic on the planet, become part of the collective misunderstanding as quickly as one can pass a ballot or look across the room to catch an agreeable nod from kin or friend. In essence, the resolution of social and intellectual confusion prompts an undereducated election of popular knowledge into the category of truth.

She lost patience with words and leaned over to tell him to cover one eye. She then asked him, "Can you see all of me?"

Mick looked around at his roommates. They laughed collectively at him, as if they all knew the answer.

"Alright," Lola answered for him, "you could have said: with one eye, I can see all surfaces of your body that are exposed to me in an artificial two-dimensional neuronal rendition of the molecular excitations that are occurring on the surfaces of your body and the conjugated molecules that stain your clothes.

And given that the substrate of my perception is some fucked up kind of horizontal and vertical on and off switches all mapped into my visual cortex, I'm seeing all the on and offs, and they seem to represent a picture of you that looks just like it looks right now."

"But you didn't say that, unfortunately," Lola evaluated. "But let me ask you one question. It appears to the anatomists that your eye is perfect and you can see everything in the field, but it also appears to the anatomists that there is a part of the retina that has no capacity to perceive. That is, there is a part of your retina, in the back of your eye, where the optic nerve transmits information to the brain. It just so happens, though, that right where the optic nerve hits the retina, where it gathers all the millions of minuscule electronic signals that you eventually understand as seeing something, it just so happens that there are no photoreceptors at this point where the nerve and the retina connect."

"So, Mick, I ask you, if you cover one eye, can you see all of my body?"

He covered one of his eyes and gave her a lewd whole-body analysis.

"Sure, I still can, but I didn't understand a word of what you just said."

"Let me put it simply, Micky boy. You have a blind spot. In both eyes. There is one part of your eye that sees nothing, nil, absolute zero because there is no information gathering at one point in the back of your eye."

"So what, I can still see all of your body. I can tell describe for you the color of every single square inch of your body right now."

"Alright, let's try this not with my body, but with a simple diagram."

Lola whipped out some of her trusty notebook paper, which she used for writing down events in her life that she considered important. She also used it for rolling joints. The one and the other were mutually necessitating. She grabbed a pencil from the table and drew a simple diagram:

$$+ \qquad\qquad \bullet$$

She held the paper a few feet from his face and instructed him to look only at the perpendicular lines.

"Can you see these two objects with one eye covered?"

"Sure, I see 'em."

She brought the paper slightly closer.

"Still see them?"

"Yep, I see 'em, this is stupid."

She brought it a little closer to his eye, now about a foot away from his face.

"Still see them both?"

"What the hell did you do, use disappearing ink?"

"So, you can't see both?"

"No, the stupid circle disappeared."

Lola moved the paper back a little, and Mick could again see the black circle, and he looked at her.

"Now I ask you again, looking at me with one eye, can you see my whole body? Huh, blind man?"

His brow was wrinkled up like an occluded continental shelf, the skin on his forehead igneous, the layers of his skin metamorphosing into a slightly different conception of the world. He fought back with optimism.

"So what? Who cares if my eyes miss stuff from time to time? I can still think and be relatively sure what I see and make decisions based on what I see. I mean, you can't tell me that this so-called blind spot can conjure people, make me believe I saw someone do something, or drastically alter my observation of the world as it is. Don't tell me that if I can't make out the colors of a girl's dress, then it will make me do something differently. And that's all we care about, right, what we do while we're here on this planet?"

Mick's questions remained rhetorical. Lola lit up a fresh joint. The roommates remained skeptical about Lola's rantings. They all looked around the room for a little while, glancing deeper into framed paintings of blues musicians they admired, peeling yellow paint on the walls and light brown handprints at all major traffic points, a gaping wet, smoky hole in the corner of the living room the upstairs tenant's leaky heater had been silently working on over the past few years, and a coffee table lathered with orange paint and laced with sofrito rice, salsa, and marijuana stems, which was at a particularly comfortable height for putting legs upon, all bathed in micro shards of broken glass and bleached sand from an hourglass that cracked one night in the midst of roommate lunacy,

Mick hanging on the ceiling with rock climber grip on the dental molding above the doorway, Michael upside down in a handstand on a plastic chair that subsequently collapsed and sent him off into a pile of foul black garbage bags, Brady playing "All You Need Is Love" on the kazoo with his legs behind his head suspended in the air by his straightened arms on the floor, and finally the dog, excitable, barking, attention-hungry, paws on the table in a desperate act to keep up with the feats, a last yelp of a bark and her impatience turned into physical disturbance, a nudge of the hourglass, teeter to and fro which Mick noticed but not in time to dismount from the ceiling, the glass sheath crashed onto the far edge of the table, released the watchful sands all over the apartment and forever marked it with the limits of time.

CHAPTER 9
Lola Mail's a Letter

Lola walked slowly to a mailbox. She contemplated briefly whether or not what she was doing was right or wrong. She then, again briefly, contemplated going to a library, looking up some books on morality and the covenant between people, pondered the existence of true qualities and the nature of pure selfishness and human nature. She thought she might read long works regarding qualities such as truth, honesty, and the golden rule. But at the end of the day, she felt that she was right. She was doing unto others as she wished others would do unto her. She had done it before. When she was young, she had pondered romance, the nature of words, and the power of the written word. She willed her dreams into existence because she lacked the good life she had always wanted, and wanted to make others happy because the feelings inside of her were not as pleasant as she wished.

She mailed the letter after kissing it on the stamp. She felt good, very good about what she had done, and ran away with a smile and smoked a cigarette.

CHAPTER 10

Upper West Broadway

Upper West Broadway glimmered, hokey and empty as ever, but necessary. All the electricity seemed to drain to right here. Automatons danced to the whim of unrelenting theater bulbs, blinking in some algorithm of insanity. The clear and bloodshot eyes walked by each other, one of them against the grain, the to and fro of a local existence. Freshly-filled bread-shop shelves scoffed at the sweaty delicatessen meat across the street. Piles of dog shit on the pavement are worthy of contemplation. The unhoused people in the area had chosen particular squares of concrete which they knew were heated from below by cauldrons of greed. They seemed to be involved in an intellectual pursuit, completely absorbed in a monologue that had no end in sight, and happy to have chosen a life of abstraction, irresponsible in no one's eyes.

Blythe walked on.

The route took him a few blocks east of the main strip. The darkness here was thematic, suggestive of scripted murder, cinematic poverty. But the backdrop was real. The scent of murder hung impossible in the air. Poverty lay in the street, run over by cabs and limos, and police cars. It hid the unseen like an accomplice in the crimes of the city government. The phone booths drove you to slam the meaty, brittle handsets when you lost your change, which you almost always did. Malfunction predominated. Kyle thought about how he might be the one who rips the receiver from the payphone one day—he saw them dangle from time to time, wondered what might lie behind such a statement. He could be kicked out of his apartment and so quickly, so suddenly, be so much a part of the street that he was glad to stay friendly with the residents of the pavement and gave them food and money from time to time.

A plague of rats kept consumption at a minimum. At the dinner table, the languorous youth dreamed not of excess lying in wait in the refrigerator, but of the myriad teeth in the mouth of a plump city rat, well-fed on rinds and grizzle. None lost profit from the skittish feet and fluttered hearts of boys and girls who were frightened by the black missiles self-thrusted in and out of the garbage, only to disappear into the entrails of the buildings through unlikely holes.

He saw a woman ahead, a few moments in front of him. The cold night sent a shiver through his wet insides. Despite his raw red face, sockets ablaze, and ears that rang from the noise of the city, he could make out her features quite clearly from afar. She wore a long, colored robe that hung down along frail, bloodless legs. The robe covered her entire body and the ground, and as they headed towards each other in the middle of the night, the robe seemed to hover on the fresh dew and dark, greasy cement.

He saw her coming closer, within interactive distance, a stone's throw away for a man like our friend Kyle. "She might say nothing to me, give me as much attention as a street lamp," Kyle presumed. "At best, a glance or a forced smile." His heart pounded heavily in his chest as is usual when about to confront someone. His lips verged on each other, and a noise began down in the disrepair of his belly, and just when a kind comment, an evening "hello," was making its way into his maw, instead, she broke the silence. Her gelatinous mouth opened wide upon him, strings of her driest spit stretched from upper to lower incisor, and immediately following an inimical glare, she said right to his face: "White boy, you got no business bein' in Harlem, what the fuck you doin' here?"

She walked away, as if she had made her feelings clear.

"I should just shrug it off and walk home," he thought aloud to himself. Nothing would come of it. No remorse, no changed ideas. "I shouldn't even listen to her," he said. But despite the mockery, his inconvenient existence at this moment, it was possible to walk away from her. No retort. No retribution. His senses were dull, and his throat too dry to speak anyway. He could only force himself to glance at her over his shoulder. He touched his hot face and furrowed eyebrows. He felt about as he normally did: dejected, embarrassed at having stepped onto the street.

From a cliff-like outlook on a haggard wall of stones far above the street, a young girl no more than seven years of age wondered what Kyle and this woman had in common. She was perched on a metal fence with stick-bone hands poked through in imitation of a shackled prisoner she had seen on television. She watched them pass in the night, noticed not quite consciously that there had been some exchange, a transfer of information from one to the other. She could not put her finger on it, though.

What such a young child saw as an unrelated couple passing each other in the middle of the night—what she chalked up to randomness, uncertainty, the massiveness of the earth, or the funky ways of gravity, and saw as merely another minuscule dropping in a grandiose pile of horseshit—was actually the rebirth of a disturbed man's life. But his disturbance has no meaning to a child. No more does a child sense the weight of the future than does the surging pool of wax atop a burning candle, burgeoning up and roundish and finally pouring out over the melting rim where it establishes the continual drip. And not until it has dripped for hours and hours does it pile up to form a foundation—a work of art, really—of solidified thoughts.

She had no idea, though. She just wanted to go home and see her mother. She stuck her finger deeper in her ear and climbed a few rungs higher in the fence to keep a lookout for other happenings down below.

Looking around, the surroundings that Kyle normally took as repetitious nothingness immediately snapped into richness. Sanctity seeped from the bare city street. The pavement, sweat, and pitiful windows forced foul breath upon the airways between the buildings. His feet—what wonderful movable feet he had acquired—bathed in gray dust and soot and ash, which all made their way into his pant cuffs. His step rolled quickly now on his once-rotten path, the memories of his former conceptions barely a wake in the film on the city street.

To the north, pristine aluminum fences atop an already insurmountable wall of rock stood straight and senseless, protecting the church from a poor area of heathens—or perhaps to prevent the zealots from falling to their death. Burnt streetlights colored the scene in a vaporous golden brown. To the south, tired facades spiked with green paint peeled away like an unwilling infant. In the park to the northwest, the grassy fields were quiet, mutilated by perverts, marauders, and myths.

Kyle didn't think he was in Harlem. He had been in Harlem many times before, and people did not say that kind of thing in Harlem.

Harlem. He said it to himself several hours later, deep in his most guttural of throats, many, many times in succession, relegating the word to its constituents: a soft throaty beginning, a bog of a middle, and a vibrating lip at the end.

By repeating the sound so many times, he changed the word's meaning. He altered its importance, the fact that it signified a place, a physical location. He stole essence, power, and fear. He reduced the word to a sound, and the sound fizzled like a bottle rocket dud, instilling quiet excitement, then reaching an apex and falling towards the ground where it would make no sound as it hit a bed of grass, worms, and dirt. He took from this place, whose boundaries were not so well defined, the fright of a place where the sidewalks fall into the street and the buildings breathe smoke.

He turned the corner onto his street, only a few blocks away. He reached the apartment front door, fumbled with the lock with hands like wooden clubs from oxygen deprivation, dropped his coat to the floor, and collapsed on the couch, a poisoned man.

The apartment was as empty as ever, though he couldn't recall why the chair was knocked over. The room reeked of cigarette smoke and Mexican food. The roommates had been here recently. So had the dog. The food containers were all licked cleaner than a military urinal.

He turned his head on its side and looked out the sullen windows on the far side of the room. The tops of street lights were just visible, which Kyle used to think were good things, beneficent markers of a neighborhood concerned with the safe nighttime ambulation of its citizens. As he stared, they shifted and changed. Their sharp black metal curves turned into malevolent design. They threatened to expose weakness, interpret secret looks. They dared you to throw rocks at their lights or to climb their greasy, unkempt poles. They tried their best to scrape you with their raw metal.

It would be a good time for a run, even a sprint. To run as long and as far as possible. He wanted to cough out all the smoke, exhaust, and dust that he had inhaled so far in life, to purge the past, but he could not find the energy to do so, and wanted to feel like someone feels after they've contemplated ending their life.

The next night, Kyle was in a giddy mood. He spent the whole day thinking about the previous night. He felt the need to walk down the same block at around the same time. In fact, he made it a repeat night. A real kicker. He even thought of consuming the same type of gin. And the same amount at the same rate. "Ha, she will see, I even ate the same meal at the same time," he said to himself. "I will get back at that woman. I'll show her it's not that easy to throw such an exclusive insult at me and think she can change my life."

It was easy to walk down the street the next night. His feet felt just fine, removed from his usual corporeal heaviness and pain. The back was limber, and he was almost overwhelmed by an odd sense of lightness. No one noticed him, though. He felt like he could almost walk right through people. He dared not look left or right and chance an interruptive glance from a stranger. He walked down the street this perfectly replicated night in total silence, happy with his stride and confident leg motion. "A mist of confidence hangs around me," he almost said aloud, and in the process amused himself severely, so much that a low, contemptuous laugh erupted from the shallow regions of his belly.

He eyed a middle-aged woman a little way in front of him. She appeared to be on a stroll as well, but what a meaningless stroll. A walk for transportation. How senseless she must have felt! Kyle hustled down the block, again on a cold, dark night, at a brisk tempo, about ten yards behind the woman. He imagined that it would be good fun to shout to her, "Run away, lady. Run away from me because I am confidence incarnate, and you should run away. I make you feel anxious and inconsolable." But he sensed a panic in her tempo, the type you use when moving an uncomfortable amount of laundry.

To Kyle's surprise, she ducked away into a dilapidated residence on the south side of the street. As he was passing the door, she looked back out at the street and almost fogged up the window with her breath. The mistrust, almost fear now was quite apparent in her eyes. She looked not just at the outside, not at the street, but at Kyle Blythe, as if all his hustling had been to get to her, not just to get home and rest his gin-reddened cheeks, but to catch up for some malicious event. The previous brisk pace slowed as he took a glance behind him to see if anyone else had seen what had apparently taken place. It was in vain. He turned towards the residence and pranced up to the front door, took a look through the melted fingerprints—his brow bunched up on his forehead—to see if she lingered, though quite afraid of seeing her, only to discover that she had disappeared into an intimidating world.

As his eyes adjusted to the heinous yellow fluorescent light of this particular stoop, still agaze through the wire-mesh laden glass, he caught sight of something so horrible to him that dizziness struck him rapidly. He faltered. His legs gave way as his eyes rolled up in his head, bobbing to and fro, a meager ship in a harsh sea. He fell backward onto his ass with enough left to save his head from hitting the steps. The stoop ran out, and he rolled sideways down a few short stairs onto the sidewalk. Grains of sand and pebbles raked into his hands, and a chewed lollipop stick sugar-glued itself onto the left flap of his jacket. No one was there to help him up.

What he had seen was torturous. Or tortured. Sidewalks and concrete pavement did not have the reflective properties of glass, which he enjoyed for a moment while still face down, safe. What he had seen was his own image. A depiction of himself he was not ready for, the doubly fuzzy face of a man totally unfamiliar with itself, a face razed of meaning to its owner, a total lack of recognition, a face of silliness absent for months, of seriousness unknown for years, of true laughter forgotten. What he saw was his own face with strange hair, a brow wrinkled like dirty sheets, a black hole of a mouth without a visible tongue, pernicious eyes drugged downwards, ill-fitting eyebrows waxy and dead, a nose bereft of function, for it did not sense anything. What he saw was a forehead lost deep in the mind of a self-contemplative hermit, and lips tucked away in a frown, a spasm of perception, unreal. A face afraid of life, really, tortured by the lack of reward he had undergone for several years now, his expectations diffuse and mangled like a carcass in a field.

Kyle was not the type to get noticed, especially on the lost streets of the city. He had rarely sensed this type of apprehension anywhere near him. He had never been to war. He had never even been anywhere near violence. He had never sensed any kind of fear caused by him. If he were to really think about it, he had barely even experienced strong emotions.

When he got home, a mere two blocks further on in time, the realization that these two events took place at almost exactly the same place on that very street, at almost exactly the same time of the night—four o'clock in the morning—struck him in the face like the brunt of some cruel joke.

Loneliness conspired on the way up the stairs, all the way to the fourth floor. The hurtfulness of her actions seemed more painful with each step, and several times he began to float back downward, stopping himself only with the railing. His eyes teared with humid frustration. His breath heated up, eyes almost popped out from the pressure. He passed black gouges on the stairwell walls, the inevitable sign of the itinerant tenancy of city buildings. At least they had their furniture with them. Eventually, he slipped away from the worn marble of old stone steps, the smoky doors that hid neighbors and all their frightening smiles. The confusion started to get to him.

Kyle Blythe could not accept defeat. He wanted to grab that lady by her sweaty palms and ask her if she really had been running from him. Her eyes had looked wide and alert. Her body sensed danger. Could she possibly have been running from our Kyle? Could she ever have dreamed that he would steal her belongings, or her keys, enter her home, and destroy whatever she had inside?

Several days later, a little boy spat right at him, on the pavement right in front of his feet! Then the little innocent stared at Kyle with empty eyes. He was holding his mother's hand, and she paid attention to something else, approvingly. A little boy who could not have been more than seven years old!

"What have I become?" Kyle wondered. "How could this be true and happening to me?"

If he was going to do something, he had to do it fast. A day in Kyle's eye lasted no longer than the furtive stroke of an owl's wing. A good coffee runs cold as a snowflake melts on a hand. He could not work his life away, drink away his nights and weekends, and let this woman direct the entire future towards the path it was currently heading down, rife with dejected glances, sunk faces, and thoughts of doom.

She had made a strange difference in his night. She had obliterated something in him, something that classified his existence. Before: illness, bah; loneliness, part of a normal man's life; malefaction, a necessary evil. But she had been outright rude to him, something no one had done for years. In fact, no one had spoken directly to him for some months now.

Shrouded by his illness and misery for so long, he had forgotten that it did not come from within.

CHAPTER 11

Waking Up

In the morning, he woke late. Late for work, that is. He waved a comb through his rough hair and grabbed the bus. Despite the rush, he felt better than he had in the past few tumultuous days. All the questions faded away. He felt more aware of everything. He had to get to work, which was terribly depressing at the moment, after a weekend.

City life had crackled to a crisp standstill. Fumes from the hot buses blasted headward. Arms hung dead, too frozen to wave. A forlorn worker's face, an exhausted woman with two red-faced children, yet now and then a storefront wide open.

Luckily, Blythe worked up a cool sweat, not the hot kind that wore on his soul. It kept him preoccupied with body matters until moments before the draconian monster on the East side. Most days, he could hold off thinking about work until just milliseconds before he entered the lab. Lately, he had been unhappy with his work, running uninteresting experiments that promised to yield nothing other than proof that someone was working on something. Productivity did not necessarily require practical results in a research lab. Anyways, he was really there for the people. Sure, he wanted to help cure illness, but he was only a technician; any old scrub can do the things he did routinely.

It suffices to say he only needed a reason to move on to something else, something more inspirational.

It was the Lower East Side. The thought alone of Maker's Mark and its sour throaty wince had already inebriated Blythe and his rare friends by the time they sauntered into the bar, lapsed into a wooden table near the entrance they had warmed with pathetic asses a hundred times. They stayed away from most other kinds of alcohol and its red-nosed owners with their gnarly teeth and breath of coal mills. Beer was fine. Beer drinkers were, for the most part, hearty folks, scientists and humanitarians, environmentalists and graduate students. Crooks and winos kept their distance from beer; must be the warm, distended belly they're afraid of, the bloated-belly burps, crinkled cans, bottle jingles which are so overwhelming if you're intent on misery.

A cold wind kept them awake. An annoying awareness of every woman that walked through the door hung around like a sudden fog. It would not be accurate to say that they talked to each other; they were talking to each other's turning heads, their eyes drawn by the looks of others that made chipped glasses run dry all too quickly. Kyle had no idea what he was thinking, but he convinced them to head out to the bar she frequented when she had lived in the city. She had failed to mention where they would go, and she hadn't called, but he thought if she was in the city, she would go there.

They were not far. Swanky and drunk, they made their way without a soul of interruption. There, now in morose, unbalanced moods, they discovered that all the women had someone to dance with. Kyle smiled, imperceptible, near a couple making out at the bar. He was almost happier to watch people make out with their partners. At least someone was doing it, enjoying a kiss or a dance, to keep it alive. "All You Need Is Love" by the Beatles crept into his head and wouldn't leave. He guzzled beer, chewed a lime, and ordered another. He pictured himself asleep at the bar, head on the bar, bloodshot eyes, and sheer sleepy ferocity.

He wobbled a few times. He looked around, sensed an awareness of his own face, which said I am lonely.

He wasn't even going to say goodbye to his friends. They did the same thing; it's understood.

He was on his way out the door when she grabbed him from behind and pulled him over to the bar.

She said, "Surprised seeing you here." She didn't say why she hadn't called.

"I just got in tonight," she said. Kyle said very little.

She appeared shocked by Kyle's presence, as if she had never thought she would see him on this trip to New York. She had written the letter after all, hadn't she? She came so close to misinterpreting the silly grin on his face as contentedness, and Kyle hated it since it hid his anger so well.

It was a British guy standing next to her, idling the change in his pockets, as if to say to Kyle, "See, I've got more money in change in my pockets than you've got in your bank account." You dumb shit for losing her, how could you let that happen? She's such an amazing woman. Kyle could tell by the way he wore his pants that she was not really in love with him. He knew the kind of guy she wanted, not a grungy type and most certainly not a pants to the belly button preppy tightwad like this fucking guy. He assumed they had been having sex and would have sex later that night. She may or may not have wished at that moment to be back with old Blythe, but he wasn't about to give her any choice, so he pulled her away from the limey. He started to follow, but a look from Kyle and a hand gesture sent him back to the bar. He leaned on the bar and left them alone, then went to the bathroom, or some other idiotic place.

To understand the dead heartedness that was the chest of Kyle Blythe was a difficult task for her. He pulled out some old tactics, quick, random kisses that he had done once in high school, caught her off guard because she had been avoiding the first kiss for weeks. It worked back then. She had smiled and requested many more impromptu kisses. The kiss that was attempted under the cover of a loud group of smokers was not well-received. All he could do was hope that she wasn't really as resentful as she pretended when he tried again to kiss her and tell her that he loves her. She said, "he treats me better than you ever did." She put her hand to the side of his face and tried to comfort him.

One of those lines that sticks for a long time.

The disparities here were mind-blowing for Blythe. The letter. What about the godforsaken blimy letter? Why had she written it so formally and addressed him so persuasively, if he was a millionaire being sought by a bunch of broke bankers looking to fund their hemorrhoidectomies? Something did not make sense to Blythe.

He abandoned these thoughts. He was too broke to take a cab and too sick of people to take the subway. Four desolate miles later, he was at his apartment door.

Fully clothed, shoes still on with a cigarette butt embedded in the tread, Blythe woke. For all he knows, he must have been eating cigarettes instead of smoking them. A hand on the wall was needed to stay in the upright position. The clock said 6:23, with the PM light illuminated.

For a moment, he thought of himself as merely a part of a huge equilibrium; death and life acted at about the same rates, with death always just a little in the lead. What was he to do, cherish each moment and live as he wants, perform his duties and accomplish everything he wants, and yet nothing? Whatever Kyle thought of himself at that moment, with the alarm clock blaring twelve hours too late, his hands rubbing legs that had been with him since the very beginning, lungs chock full of biota, it felt like an end was coming all too soon.

Nebulous is the only word to describe the ensuing day. Nebulous, as in hard to talk about, unformulated, as in a large cloud of interstellar gas and dust with more mass and electric charge than our entire solar system.

From the entrance to Blythe's apartment, you can see the place where a jealous boyfriend took his ex-girlfriend's life with his own hands. He killed her in the cover of night. Soon after, Con Edison or some other geniuses installed brighter lights near this very spot. It should not be long before Central Park is one big titillating ball of light bulbs. Come to think of it, we might as well save the electricity; no fool, safe in a cozy apartment, would dare to call the police if they by chance heard someone being raped or robbed or killed. Then again, the lights are convenient because now you can see people letting their dogs shit all over the place at night.

After nursing a painful hangover with coffee practically intravenously and treating ashtray mouth with cranberry juice, he made his way to work and quit his job. His boss had always told him that he had nothing without his health, and even though she confused Blythe's metaphor about burning candles at both ends with some kind of retirement ceremony, she was very understanding about letting him part from the lab. She offered him a position at any time if he wished to return, for which Blythe was grateful.

Blythe cooked for three days straight, nodding off at times while the oven was filled with lasagna. On the fourth day after quitting his job, he decided that he might want to teach people how to read for a living. The next day, that idea was as gone as if it never existed. He gave up on several other things and declared himself a musician. Fifteen years of playing the drums should get him somewhere, but he liked to read too much to do that. On the fifth day after quitting his job, he made a solid decision. He decided to forget about making a decision and do whatever it was that pleased him at any time.

Days later, just sitting around doing nothing but thinking about what he felt like, Blythe rushed to the kitchen to pull out a drawer full of menus. He felt the need to be a full-time waiter in a restaurant, get money in tips, and keep the cash right away. For some reason, looking at the menus helped him to think this through. He dwelled on it for an afternoon, then figured it was perfect for the time being. Zero commitment, except to satiety. Zero responsibility except to bring the beer before the foam goes away, a hamburger before the bun goes hard under the warmer.

He made his way to the restaurants lining Broadway one by one, menu by menu, and application after application. Of course, he had a little experience in the arena of burritos and enchiladas, but the market for those was quite limited on the Upper West Side, so he settled for a crappy restaurant with American cuisine, baby back ribs, and burgers. Work started the same day he went in to apply. That's the way he likes it. If he wants something, he wants it when he wants it. Other things are worth waiting for, but for some things that are material in nature, for example, a piece of tape to hold a page together, it is best to acquire them right away.

CHAPTER 12

Didier Fontaine

Didier Fontaine woke quietly to the sound of the slow brushing of teeth in the bathroom. He rolled over and stared lazily at the light emanating from above the door. It spilled over into the dark room and lit up most of the ceiling. For the first time since moving in, He noticed what a fine job the crew did on the ceiling, specifically in plastering the joints between the sheets of drywall. Not one line showed where the tape was run, and where the screws were laid. A thin, even coat of paint lay flat along the entire ceiling, and he thought that another way of doing that would be to cut out the whole ceiling and dip it in a can of paint the size of a swimming pool. With this image, he closed his eyes.

Meghan finished brushing her teeth and closed the door. Oversized images flooded Didier's brain; hexagons, squares, and obtuse shapes came rushing at him at incredible speeds, growing in size as they approached his perspective, and more appeared as soon as they disappeared noiselessly into his field of dreams. Tight shapes morphed into globular masses, which continued to move fast towards him. He tried opening his eyes to make it stop. When he closed them, the images returned.

The water in the bathroom started to run abruptly. He imagined her clothes falling off her hips onto the floor, where they made a sound that sent a quiver through the bedridden Fontaine, and he heard her first steps into the shower. The water was quieter. Thoughts of the long day ahead forced him to tuck the covers under his legs and put his face into the pillow for one last bout of heavy sleep before the looming day began. Sunlight had not yet touched the bedroom, and that was the last thought of Didier's before she came out of the bathroom partly dressed.

"Are you tired?" she asked energetically. "Why don't you just take the day off? You need some rest."

Didier woke slowly, not remembering for a moment that he had fallen asleep. "If I took the day off, there'd be a whole crew of people that would be there…waiting for me." She sat down on the bed beside him. He took her hands and grasped them on top of his chest. "They can't work today without me. No one else can lay a semi-circular wall." As he spoke, he shaped her hands into a semicircle. They both stared at the hand structure for a moment. The last day Didier took a day off was a month and a half ago. He was currently the best mason in all of Paris. And the youngest. He laid natural stone faster than any other, and with the current demand for stone structures in certain quarters of Paris, this meant that he had to do it even faster. A two-story fireplace in a day. A heart in the morning. An exterior of a home in a few days. He was paid well for his work.

"You're going to work anyway. We can spend tonight together."

"I work tonight also."

"Well then, take the night off. Can't you…"

They released hands, and she continued to get dressed. Didier got out of bed in slow motion and gave her a hug. They kissed with staggered, clean lips for a few moments, and she pushed herself away, threw on a shirt, and was out the door. It was 5:23 AM, and He got in the shower.

In his pre-Lola days, Didier Fontaine was lost. Lost in drugs, risky sex, and pain. Three lumbar disc herniations and a few sloppy surgeries had left him with a nasty narcotic habit. He tried to console himself with women, which had always been easy for him.

Then one time, he met a fun-loving artistic girl, not his usual type, at the Jardin de Luxembourg. Actually, she picked him up, literally. She had been sitting on a bench knee-deep in the harm of plastic and her version of environmentalism with a group of German exchange students, while he was passed out on the bench next door, half-naked at the dead end of a four-day binge.

Lola took him under her wing, detoxed him with a combination of hash, Woody Allen movies, and placebo Valium sugar pills. The hash, she knew, was not such a good idea as one bad habit begets another, but it worked after all. When he had finished with all that, smelled a bit better, and had swallowed whole a good meal of pan-fried sausages, pasta, and basil, she had what is commonly referred to as hot sex with him, one of his rewards for getting off prescription drugs.

Fontaine wasn't even French. His parents grew up in Long Island, Carle Place to be exact, and had a long-standing shared psychotic delusion that they were, in fact, from France, while they were both born in Cook County, Illinois, solidly documented on their birth certificates. His mother, Joanna Fontaine, changed her name to Joan, then contemplated "Joan de" as a first name, but then decided she would receive many letters to Joan D. Fontaine, which would infuriate her enormously. She almost succeeded in secretly changing her husband's name, Henry, to Henri, but stopped when the F.B.I. came upon her name after they busted a passport operation in New York. She had bought a French passport under the name Joan de Fontaine, born in Paris in 1942, birth records lost under the Nazi occupation, as they told her to say. She even watched some old French films and could easily recount the story of how her father recalled standing up at a table in a restaurant where they wouldn't let Jews eat and denounced the French officers who were complicit with Hitler's regime. It was, of course, a scene from a movie.

Both his parents died in a car accident in 1999 on the way to see a showing of the original 1960s version of "A Bout de Souffle" at a theatre in Ronkonkoma. They were wearing berets and all. Didier buried his mother in a beret with a statue of the Eiffel Tower in her hand. He placed it in her hands himself; the cold rigor had startled him, and he nearly passed out.

He inherited quite a fortune, save for a few hundred thousand dollars his mother lost to a con artist on craigslist.org offering partial ownership to L'Arc de Triomphe in Paris.

Didier, whose name was David on his birth certificate, kept the name as a reminder of his parents. He also visited France in his early twenties, shortly after they died, as a tribute to them. He got so hooked on their wine, cheese, and laid-back lifestyle that he stayed there. After a dinner at Chili's on the Champs-Elysées alone one night, he took the satisfaction of carving "Joan et Henri étaient ici" on a bench near the Arc de Triomphe. He only felt close to his parents in Paris.

He had a hell of a flat for a good few years and a roaring life in his twenties, and blew through a few hundred thousand that he had planned for his stay overseas. When said budget ran out and his liver was almost kaput, the rest of his inheritance locked away in an estate, he started working for a mason under Lola's conviction that it would bring him closer to the earth and the environment. Basically, it was Lola's final step in his detox. It worked.

CHAPTER 13

"Yeah, man, it's the serendipity, you know? It's the uncanny bro, right in your head. It's like an open door, and once it's been opened, you can't help but look into this world…a world of déjà vus, coincidences, ghosts, faith."

Blythe sipped beer from a glass that stuck to the maple-brown bar, feet also glued to the bronze footrest below. He sipped constantly because a ranting person next to him made him uncomfortable. Darren wasn't there for him. He needed someone who had in mind Blythe's history of alternating exuberance and downtroddenness. He needed a friend, not a rotten drunk rambler with a nasty scar on his face.

Glance at a girl who was dancing on the bar. Her feet seemed never to touch the oak. She already returned the glance.

"You say faith, though. I can't stand…"

"No, faith and religion have gotten a bad name over the years. Religion is on the right track, you know, but it's just not running in the same race."

Blythe hated the way he used clichés.

"Man, you don't even need faith, you just need to open your eyes. No, not even your eyes. There's nothing to see. There are no Dead Sea Scrolls, bro, you know. Just…just the serendip and your own perception, man. That's it."

Someone said her name was Angelina. The annoying guy sensed his interest in the dancer. He started to bring her into the discussion, saying that she was magical and some other bullshit, that it was obvious that she had a good spirit, more than just a normal person. And Kyle would never quite get this guy's theories, nor why he took his word for the Golden Truth on this steamy night, latched onto his fantasies as his own, whereas in former days he would have stayed as far away from his ramblings as he would a gutter in a city ravaged by plague. An askew face, beady eyes, the man resembled a pirate. He gulped alcohol, smoked readily.

There was something so easy about his man's life, Blythe wanted to feel a part of it.

Later, Angelina said—laying on her back with Kyle's hands performing—that she did not believe in spirits or any forces other than those that fell under contemporary or theoretical physics. She believed that a coincidence is just a coincidence, and most of the time, a derivative of sleep deprivation. "Dogs have dreams too," she said. Her dog's blood-red eyes seemed half open at times, even while she chases phantom bunnies in phantom fields of warm, shining wet snow and brown grass as her eyes flutter at random and her paws run in space.

Kyle caught her eyes by the dim bar light, and she pulled him over to her. Blythe had iron lungs, and she was an electromagnet. As he approached her, his step unsure, his shoelaces untied, his lungs alchemized into ferrous flesh, his heart began pumping molten lead tachycardic, and his stomach erupted into a cupric acidic frenzy. He rapidly morphed from a leaden stoic into a phlegmatic, pulsing, pumping, self-digesting biological reality. She had the eyes of a seasoned bar drinker. He tried to say something, but his lip turned to jelly the minute she changed posture, sat up straight to a position that seemed ready to be lifted from her chair and taken away to somewhere utterly pleasant. He barely got out a word, and his palms were cold and sweaty.

"Hi, my name's Kyle."

No response, though she sipped a martini.

"I just thought you looked like…"

"I know. I wanted you to come over. Here, wait a minute…"

She stood up quickly, making her way through the molasses crowd. Seconds later, Blythe fell into a chair she wrestled from acquaintances. He faded away into the scene of the bar, leaned back to get a cigarette from his pocket, and still had his hand in the pocket when she leaned over and pressed her mouth against his. It was a definitive kiss, one that left old Blythe reeling and sensing that he would do many silly things to try to be with this woman more often. Sticky lipstick, love-drunk, he put his hand on her warm cheek. One finger found the lobe of her ear—ah, the ear—and they kissed for a few minutes. She pulled away. They both sat down, staring straight ahead into what seemed an empty room, when there were hundreds of people in it.

Kyle broke the silence: "Have you ever seen a dog in the middle of a dream, with its paws running and its tongue hanging out like…"

"Of course," she interrupted, "Livvy does it all the time. It's funny to think about, because it makes me think that dogs must have very complex brains. If Livvy's brain has developed a system to occupy itself even while the paws and tongue are paralyzed, then it must be quite complicated."

"Livvy's your dog?"

"Livvy is wonderful. She's totally used to me now. She used to think I was a slob. Oh, of course it's not my dog. I just happen to live with her."

"That's funny. I mean, you can't really own anything. You just have the responsibility of storing and taking care of it. Anybody else can do whatever they want with whatever it is; it just so happens that we've made some...some laws that punish people for storing or taking care of my stuff."

Her eyes smiled. "How'd we go from kissing to dogs to your theory of property ownership?"

"That's a good question. It seems so necessary, though. Do you see how that was necessary?"

"No, what seems so necessary?"

"You, me, us meeting here. This bar. These people. How could this very moment be any different? We're here now. We've lived up till now, and each and every moment has been distinct...each moment has happened. How can anything else be true? It can't. What happens happens. What..."

She cut him off, "I agree, but when we look back at things, sometimes one person has a different take on it than another person, like a reporter, for example, has a million different details that could be told on each aspect of everything reported..."

"Right, that's different. How we deal with an event doesn't mean the event didn't happen in some exact way. Alright, to get really technical, you could trace the path and course of each and every electron and proton and element and molecule, knowing exactly what neurons were firing in whose brain, knowing exactly the momentum of each part of everything, and we could trace that and recreate it if we tried hard enough, right?"

"I guess so. So, what do you want to do? Do you want to trace and recreate everything? Is that what you want?"

"No. I don't know what I want. I'm just saying that anyone who questions the truth is just not a good enough detective."

"And you're the sleuth that's gonna figure it all out?" One of those things people say that made Blythe feel awkward.

"Not by a long shot. But I am gonna show everyone how to begin. How to start…"

"What do you mean?"

"I don't know. Let's not talk about it."

"Ok, let's not talk about it anymore. Let's not talk all that much anymore, as a matter of fact. Let's just sit here."

She picked up her martini. Blythe picked up his beer.

"To not speaking," she toasted. He said nothing in return.

On the route home, a few hours later, Blythe walked right past the alleyway, Angelina next to him. They both wondered what the hell was going on, but went with it, and kept going with it late into the night until the sun rose and told them to sleep.

CHAPTER 14

Angelina never came out of the bathroom naked. Always dressed herself or wore a T-shirt. Blythe didn't think it was out of shyness. Perhaps she realized that any beauty can become less powerful if viewed too often. He was quite fond of the Proustian idea that true perception is quite brief. Catch a glimpse of someone coming out of the shower naked and wet, and then lose sight of them: that is the most revealing view. Then other days, it convinced Kyle that she might run out the door one day and never return. She had that streak in her: the type to jump into something and then freak out—because things didn't pan out the way they should have, it wasn't all she had expected, it wasn't the solution to all her questions and problems, and she could always run away from this.

For Blythe, the real kicker was finding her in bed in the morning. He ran the scenario through his head, always feeling that it was still the first night she had slept there and would probably turn out to be a prostitute, disappear in the morning with his wallet too. Those were the awkward thoughts they had entertained at one point or another. The questioning. This can't be real. They couldn't have gotten this close this soon.

Of course, all relationships involve a push to the limits of tolerance. Push your mate to the ends of their happiness, and you may get an unhindered view of what interests them. So Blythe began calling his ex-girlfriend, who by this point was probably on regular flights to Heathrow to check out locations for the reception after getting married to the English slouch she had been seeing. If they had ever been good together and would make each other happy, they would be together right now. He was probably calling her just to show her that he no longer cared for her, was no longer concerned about her. She could throw him away like a one-drag cigarette, crush his body into a severed filter and mound of ash paper and smoldering tobacco, and never regret having lit him on fire. She could light him up two seconds before hailing a Taxi, and fling him out the door milliseconds before the door shuts, nearly splitting his freshly ignited soul in two, which would lie on hard pavement until some considerate ambulator walked over the poor fellow, or a poor man picked him up and smoked without caring about what kind of smoke he got, what quality or brand he inhaled, for he has smoked all kinds and they are all the same over time. This has ceased to bother Blythe. He had learned a great deal from her, about himself and his emotions, not to mention how to regret not doing certain things.

Angelina sensed him near the phone. They had discussed his calling Meghan quite openly. He pulled the phone cord out as distant as it would go from the base of the phone: about four feet. A sexy smile on her face, with her cheeks resting on her hands, she stared and pretended to try to break his concentration. Victory was imminent, and he yelled "Stop that!" at her in the middle of dialing, then covered the phone and told her that she was just a friend. She understood that, and actually believed that too. She had once left a boyfriend in a mad rush of anger at him. But she kept calling him to talk, to ease the change from cohabitation to solitation.

"Go get some bagels or something to eat," Blythe told her obnoxiously. She replied with a contortion of the lips that said bagels are repulsive.

"From where does this...unbridled hatred for the bagel come?" he soap-boxed her. "Since when can you butter up a nice egg bagel, eat the whole thing, enjoy hours and hours of nourishment and a ton of energy, and then spit on them. Bagels are repulsive? Since when?"

Despite her unfounded wrath against the round bread, Angelina frequently consumed bagels. She filled the refrigerator with cheeses, spreads, jams, confitures, and myriad quasi-butter products. And how she filled the bathroom with things, the bathroom shelves now adorned with pink and purple and blue soaps, soaps in chips and crystals and soaps in bottles, soaps in paper and soaps in foam.

In sink corners, there were toothpastes, ring cleaners, and dental flosses. Up over the top of cabinets there were shampoos, conditioners, shampoos with conditioner, conditioners with lanolin, and baby oil, baby oil face wash, baby oil gel. Open up mirrored cabinets with defying makeups, moisture lotions, black cylinders with no label, no way to open them without know-how, foundations and powder, lip glosses, nail polishes from alien to rockstar, nail filers, nail clippers, toenail clippers, pieces of coral, pieces of mascara, vitamins for women, deodorant for women, old brick-colored glasses and a tooth. This tooth, the curious tooth that ended up in her hand one morning after yawning. This tooth, the one that solidified their relationship around the uncanny way they understood not understanding.

Blythe waited at the barbershop. To wait for the barbers, six disheveled fools before him in line, had to be the most discomforting feeling he had experienced in three months. He had been with Angelina for three months. How could it get like this? The past quarter of a year had been acceptance, wholeness, unity, solidarity compared to this feeling; the upcoming, at least as foreshadowed by frosted glass, a decapitated haircut practice dummy with a tripod body, straight black polymer hair, and gorgeous white teeth betraying a smile, promised to consist of teeth-grinding unease of stomach due to loneliness in the presence of others, and yearning for something else, someone else. It was as if Angelina were a crash test dummy. She got the job done, but he really had no feelings for her other than vague friendship and lonely lust.

CHAPTER 15

Things to Do

It started with the coffee. A sudden tingle in the belly prompted a longing for a hot cup of the black brew. Blythe spent ten minutes walking up and down a block, a few random blocks, speckled with deli after delis, one no more noticeable than the next. He crossed the street, changed his mind once, and then returned. His brow was wrinkled, and his hands were roughly stuffed in his pockets. He thought to check his hair, but it was futile in the wind. He felt ill at ease in these clothes, constantly adjusted the shirt.

Blythe finally yelled at himself and decided that any store would suffice; it's all the same in New York. But he went against that reasoning and kept walking further downtown. "Ignore the craving, put it off, so that I do not please myself too quickly, so that I do not give in to my desires too easily, without some opposition ." There was not enough opposition from the outside world when you live a life like Blythe's. Away from people, family, friends, doctors, priests, politicians, bosses, and teachers, when you are almost totally on your own, he had no idea what to do.

He had no idea which way to go, which store to buy coffee in, how much sugar was sufficient and how much milk and what kind of milk was alright to put in coffee. Will he get some disease from drinking too much of it, of anything, for that matter?

And thus it started with the coffee a slew of decisions had to be made, and preferably sooner rather than later "readjust the phone situation and the bill that I forgot to pay don't want to pay extra on that call my sister I've been ignoring her messages finally start losing a little weight get some creams or rubs or stop inhaling the city air the rashes are getting worse without anything better in sight decide what the right way to think is follow through on my goal to assert my opinions on world matters; scour international newspapers and develop ideas on global issues tell my father I love him get more memory for my computer so I can forget more look into that little gray piece of hard material that is embedded in my foot from years ago to make sure it's not cancer reread my grandfather's memoirs, organize bookshelf, remember to buy those important books that are vying for your attention in the store make Angelina happier and have better sex "

Make Angelina happier, an image of a string around a pulley, pull on one end, and the other gets shorter. It was possible to be so committed to the idea of being committed that the committee forgot what he was committed to.

For months, Blythe carried on this way, with prolonged moments each day of lost concentration. He lost himself in the city on routes that he had taken several hundred times. Got on the wrong subway lines and took buses that led him to vacant streets far from his destination. Each night, the feeling got worse as he laid by Angelina, his grasp a hand only, no warmth in it. He buried his face in the back of her shoulder, and should she want to make love, he did. But he cried afterwards in the bathroom and sat on the toilet and distracted himself with the white tiles and stared at them so long they turned into one large blob of white nothingness. He laid back down after the vertigo subsided and hoped with clenched teeth that she would just fall asleep.

CHAPTER 16

The end of the day came like a gunshot, crisp in his ears. Light leaned left, the horizon bent over, and cracked its knuckles. Blythe realized that this current life was going nowhere. He had given up on his impetuous ideas, the waitering now stale. All he saw were mouths and wallets and a colonoscopy entering the restaurant. He had lost his sense of cuisine. What he had gained, though, was weight. A few pounds a month added up. He was really quite rotund. The roommates called him Portly.

The months had moved on, a dozen or so, although hard to keep track, with or without Blythe's approval. Days were such that he longed for solemn nights, but often found himself going to things like college reunions just to avoid people. Lately, he felt better around people he didn't know. The night had passed, and he was actually enjoying himself at some Irish bar, having a few beers with two amiable women, one of whom he had apparently met in college, though he had no recollection. She had brown hair and a bland face. The main attraction was funny teeth, which are occasionally, as on her, attractive.

They wanted to leave before Blythe did, so they paid up and headed into the rain. He had envisioned an invite over to their place or to another bar, but they said goodnight and left Blythe in the rain. He ran to the corner of the street and caught some shelter under an overhang from the building above. A shaggy homeless man walked up and used the overhang also. Blythe lit a cigarette. The brown-haired girl had reminded him of her, so that he had taken a liking to her for the night. And yet he hated her. He opened a new pack of cigarettes and offered one to the homeless guy who was sharing the shelter with him, the rain still hard.

"Thanks, man," he said. "Ya know, some people ask me how I feel about panhandling. I tell 'em it doesn't matter if you got seventy-five cents in your pocket or a million dollars in the bank, as long as you wake up the next morning." He laughed with gnarly teeth, almost black. "As long as I wake up with all my arms and legs, it doesn't matter to me. My brother got diabetes, you know. They chopped his foot off. Uh uh, not me. Gonna keep walkin' and keep my armsies and legs and feet and all. Hell, I'm keeping my ding dong too, you know." The man giggled to himself and had horrible breath.

Blythe smiled, which prompted the man to ask for some change. Blythe told him that he was out of change, "gave it all away to the voluptuous bartender." He did have some change in his pocket, and ordinarily would gladly part with it, but didn't feel like it at the moment. He felt like it would have been paying him for what he said, which had entertained him enormously.

"We're all panhandlers. Some of us just sit in a bigger river than others," Blythe said in response. He didn't really think that through; it just came out. The man smiled. Blythe noticed that he already had a flattened, half-smoked cigarette behind his ear.

Without saying a word to the man aside from a wave, Kyle made his way to another local bar. He could be pretty sure to find a couple of acquaintances there, fellow hounds of the night sniffing away at the mess. He walked fast and found Ken there already with a blonde girl on his lap. She was riding him like a mechanical bull. Ken put his drink up in the air to avoid spilling, but it came off more as an imitation of the lasso technique, which Blythe appreciated uproariously. He enjoyed it so much that he sounded his presence with a hearty "Howdy y'all." Ken grabbed old Blythe with both hands on the side of his face and kissed him, prompting a weird look from his rider.

"Don't worry, sister," he assured her, "this cowboy's as straight as a bull's cock when he sees a big old heifer in heat." She laughed and continued to ride. Blythe tried to interest Ken in the notable panhandler quote, but he was too busy buying a Blythe special, gin and tonic, mostly gin.

Before they took a sip, Ken laments in a dry voice: "So I got laid off today."

"Really?" I say knee-jerk. "Ah, shit that sucks." A long pause where we both sipped at our drinks. The mechanical bulls came to rest, and she stepped down to talk to others.

"That's about the best thing that ever could have happened to you right now. You're young, you're MENSA-smart, you could do so many other things...no, forget that, go ahead, spend 12 hours a day at some money-hungry internet thing."

"Hey, there was potential at that place. It was fun and there were a lot of opportunities. I liked the people there. Mostly young people."

"What opportunities? Any opportunity to do any good for anyone?"

"I'm talking about low-tech client acquisition and sales, not program writing. The money was unreal at first. And don't give me your quasi-socialist guilt trip. I can make myself happy with money."

"Yeah, it's easy for them to pay you with money they don't have, and most likely won't have."

"True, they were downsizing, but I beat them to it."

"I thought you said you got laid off."

"Ah, whatever you call it, it still sucks."

Just then, another crew member, Gary, walked into the bar. He saw Kyle right away, and his dreadlocks looked dirtier than ever. Gary was the most rudderless man living in New York City. Kyle had concerns about his future and long-term trajectory, but he kept that to himself and continued to keep an eye on him and support his apolitical and everything lifestyle. He jumped right into a story:

"So we were driving down the FDR, maybe going 80 miles an hour in a V6 Volkswagen with 5 or 6 or 7 people, all piss drunk, minus the driver, naturally. I was leaning back, looking out the window, in a light mist of rain. Next thing I know, my neck is almost broken as we come to a slipping stop and almost hit a biker. The road was curvy, and I was mad drunk. It curved to the right, back to the left, our tires squeaked a lot, and I almost threw up. We went to Liz's, and everyone smoked pot and smoked cigarettes and listened to Lou Donaldson. I went to crash in her bed [Liz's bed]. She comes in laughing, right, hysterically. I wake up from a sweaty, hot sleep. She takes her clothes off. And then she turns on the air conditioning. Finally, I can breathe, and we get real close to each other... hey, asshole, are you listening?"

"Yeah, yeah, I'm loving it, keep going."

"till the morning when we wake up hungover."

"Wait, did you guys sleep together?"

"We slept together; that's it. She slept and I slept."

"Alright, did you have sex?"

"Shit, I can't tell you that. Anyway, we walk fifteen blocks to Owen's in Park Slope along the park in the rain. 'Bout a fifteen-minute walk, you know, you've done it before. We talked to this guy with green pants and a green truck and green shoes and even a fucking green undershirt, I swear to god, and anyways then I smoked a cigarette talking to him. Everything about him was fucking green, I swear. But that's beside the point. We walked up to his front door, and his girlfriend was in the bathroom. We went up to the roof to have a cigarette. Had a cig on the roof, talked about people we know, going places, and came back down. Wait, before we came back down, O's girlfriend came up in a sweater. Do you remember that sweater Owen puked on when you punched him in the stomach?"

I laugh too hard to answer. Before he continues, I spill my beer on the maple-brown bar. It spills over the edge. I make room for it to fall to the floor.

"That was the one with the puke hole in the back. We watched TV blindly for a while. Went to the Mexican chicken place downstairs near his house. I had roasted homemade chicken. The chicken was literally falling off the bone. Two Cokes, rice and beans, chips and dip, beans dumped all over the rice, nice and wet. Oh yeah."

An extended "Oh yeah" was the accepted signal that the story was complete.

"B minus," I said. We have this game where we tell each other the story of a day. Then we give a grade which encompasses the quality of the description, the degree of exaggeration (low points for high exaggeration levels, which are determined based on our knowledge of each other's personalities), the moral quality of the day, the decisions made that day, and the overall feeling elicited by the account. It's a pretty subjective system, but it is relatively well established.

"B minus?" he screams as if he has just been wrongly accused of murder. "But that was a great fucking night!"

"It sure sounds like it, but first of all, you didn't tell me if you had sex. Second, you forgot to tell me about the day. Third, well, there is no third; I just lost you a little in your fast pace. And that sounds dangerous, the way you guys were driving, not like a quality road trip. Remember, quality, not shock value, right?"

"Yeah, I guess you're right."

"But you got a good B for recalling a previous good day, the day I puked on Owen."

Blythe settled into the scene and started to really enjoy being sort of alone in the bar with his rare friends beside him. Maybe this could work. Perhaps he could live his life as a single man.

CHAPTER 17

"Listen, you cannot, I repeat, cannot, keep staying with her. He's headed your way. Don't forget the whole idea is here, not madness, or jealous murder or something."

I know, I know, he said. "But she really is wonderful, I mean she…"

"Alright, you see there, you're falling for her. And she's not yours to fall for. You just have to keep an eye on her, and keep her headed in the right direction, I mean, the wrong direction. You know what I mean."

He was silent for a few moments. They both were. He dragged on his cigarette while she sipped hot coffee and made a loud noise in the process.

"How are we going to get him to Paris?"

"The only way possible, like a fricking fish, lure him."

"With what?"

"I can't believe you're asking me this...you idiot...with her."

"She's not bait, you idiot."

"She's the ultimate bait. She is the bait. I mean, she is the catch. You know what I mean."

"Well, listen, I think he's actually a little too happy at this time to really, I mean, really go for her, to abandon his entire life and all his worldly possessions for her, you know what I mean? Like you were before I met you...two sheets to the wind. Listen, clearly these two are meant for each other. "

"I'll take care of that. I'll take him to..."

"Don't take him there," she cut him off. "That place is trashy."

"That's what I love about it. Works every time. Every single time, it clarifies life. And I'll have what's her face come over. Do you still have her number?"

"You know where she lives. Just look at the windows on Rue Faubourg, you'll find her."

Lola mailed a letter later that day. She spent days crafting it. She thought of every man she had ever loved, including her father, bless his soul, and tried to think of how he could lure every one of them to a certain place with words alone. What could she dangle in front of them? Promises of sex, love, happiness, and good food? All those things would probably work. But she thought for this misérable the best option would be to taunt him, which is what she did. Taunted him with losing the thing he loved, or she thought he loved.

It had to work.

CHAPTER 18

Gumption

When a seatbelt hangs out of a car, usually stuck in the passenger door, unbeknownst to driver and passenger alike, it is a sad affair, because the seatbelt will drag on and on, through rain or sunlight, wind or calm, be dragged along the rough road until eventually, little by little, the fabric is undone. Usually, no one sees this until the seatbelt is worn away into small pieces of ragged thread lining the highway shoulders wrapped around a tourist's shoelaces, or until the driver has a passenger who needs to use the seatbelt. Unfortunately, our society is organized in such a way that it is not really worth someone's time, if they had perhaps seen the seatbelt and could have predicted the damage that would have been done, to warn the driver of the minute, yet considerable, misfortune underway. Too much time is being spent here on seatbelts. This is not the subject of this chapter.

The subject of this chapter happens to be how Blythe ended up in Paris after dealing with a heavy punch of isolation and unhappiness. He had stuck himself in a bar for four years, eroded his insides with poisons, medicaments of many sorts, smokes, toxic beverages and toxic thoughts, so many bad things, as a matter of fact, that it began to eat its way inside his head. He was ignorant of what he was searching for all that time. As a matter of fact, he wasn't searching for anything. He was searching for nothing.

As for his decision to go to Paris, let's just say it was a desire, maybe even a necessity. The other day, he walked to the refrigerator to get something cold to drink; a few weeks ago a trip to the Division of Motor Vehicles to renew his driver's license; he visited a pharmacy from time to time when sick to obtain medications. If it was meat he wanted, he might stop by a butcher's shop. He loved a girl, so he went to Paris.

Blythe asked the ticket agent, in a loud voice that pierced the tired purplish-blue makeup around her eyes, "How long does it take to convince your ex-girlfriend that you're still in love with her?" The agent replied with a straight face: "About three days." So he booked a ticket for a seven-day stay in Paris. He figured the agent was a minimalist. Seven days. That should be enough. Blythe felt like he's always thought Harrison Ford characters feel most of the time.

Blythe disembarked at Charles de Gaulle at around 3 p.m. on a Monday and grabbed the train immediately to Nôtre Dame. With the best pants and cleanest shoes on, feeling like a dilapidated piece of sausage in its best cow gut, he sat on the train thinking about the people around him. A dark-haired woman with large, round eyes and light brown skin gazed straight ahead. Several black men spoke quietly at the far end of the train. He could not understand their French, though he speaks fluent French from his college days. Hip, angry youngsters stood around hanging on the poles and hitting their chests like good Frenchmen. They talked about politics in impenetrable slang.

Across from Blythe sat a disheveled man. They caught each other's gaze and couldn't help but wonder what it was that drew their eyes towards each other. Did Blythe look so obviously foreign to him? So obviously familiar? So obviously American? He saw the guy check out his pants and shoes, so Kyle checked out his. His were grungy and well-worn and contrasted with Blythe's packing job, tidy pants and shirts well creased and folded twice in half. He almost asked him how he was doing today, but withdrew. Often, extroversion from a person like Blythe was not well-received. The glint in his eye can be mistaken for lunacy; his gait a madman's; his laugh a hyena's cry. Hell, he didn't even know what language to address him in, although probably several languages would have gone over. Those damn Europeans speak so many of them.

They exited the subway. Blythe made his way to a store right away and bought a pack of Gauloises Blondes. He lit up a cigarette with a match that stayed lit in the wind. Out of the corner of his eye, he saw the strange man with grungy dungarees and rawhide boots get in a car. He gave the cathedral a cinematic look. She stared at him with her rose window, and he stared back with equal magnitude. Each pane seems to sense the glance, and he feels a bit of disdain since all three of her columns resent his presence in the country. Blythe was feeling bold. He told her aloud, first checking that no one was within hearing distance: "Fais moi la pipe, madame!" She failed to reply. In general, cathedrals don't inspire Blythe. They're just symbols of hard work. For Blythe, this particular one was a symbol of the country that had stolen the girl he loves.

The wind blew strongly on the Quai Malaquai. The walk along the wooden boards was pleasant until tiring, and he sensed just the right place to sit and enjoy the sunset. It is funny how the wind in New York blows his hair and he feels lost. In Paris, it made him feel artistic. He realized he was missing a bottle of wine, some bread and cheese.

So he rambled to a not-so-nearby market and bought a loaf of bread, fresh in the French way, Camembert, and a 7-franc bottle of wine. It took a few minutes, once back on the bridge, to find someone with a wine bottle opener, but not more than ten. It just so happened that he wanted to sell Blythe some hash ("le shit" is the expression he used), but he told him ", Je ne m'interesse plus." He finally sat down with his bread, his cheese, and his wine, cut the bread with a Swiss army knife, then spread some cheese with said knife. He took a swig out of the bottle as the cork rolled into the Seine and bobbed away quickly in the bubbly, uneven water. He imagined it was quite cold in the water. He was glad to have bread, cheese, and wine.

The sun was almost down now, but still strong enough to keep Blythe warm, and the bread and cheese were gone, along with the wine. A calm came over the area as if the others nearby were nocturnal beings, and the day-loving sides of all the people on the bridge had gone elsewhere to seek shelter, as if it were winter, and the biting cold made them seek a fire or a warm abode with family and friends.

But they had not yet left. Nevertheless, he felt alone on a bridge over a large, fast-moving river. He felt as though it was he who was moving, and not the water, and it made him want to sit down on rocky terrain that would not move for millennia, where it did not rain and where the wind did not blow for centuries, and life flourished underground between the rocks. He asked the person next to him what time it was, and she looked in his general direction. He was incomprehensible to her. She looked away, back at the sunset, without answering. He was a ghost. She had looked at him. She had heard nothing. She had seen something, the appearance of a form. She had seen an unshaven, ill-at-ease person who was obviously not French, and she had not thought it necessary to give out a simple piece of information. He abandoned the bridge and looked for his hotel.

It was not so easy for him to leave the bridge. He started to question why he had come to Paris in the first place. He was here to prove to himself and to her that he is in love with a girl, that the sole purpose of his life was not to find a mate to reproduce with, that love is real and would last, will last, that he really has emotions, and that it was possible for him to be happy in life. He was here to discover some truth. He was not here to find something.

He was here to convince himself that a certain reality was the way he thought it was.

He found the infamous Hotel de la Gare near the metro station (surprise, surprise), off the RER B line, Denfert-Rochereau stop. The proprietor was feeding his dogs (seven of them, small, big, grey, black, puffy, skinny, and stout all told) in what appears to be his living space in the basement of the hotel. Rooms were only a few dollars for the night, a few more dollars for a shower for the night, and a few more dollars for a single for the night. He splurged on the best package, which included a single room with a shower for the night. That's as long as he planned on staying. He had already bought the ticket back to New York, by way of Heathrow, on Tuesday night.

He handed over some green American bills to the proprietor of Hotel de la Gare and dragged his feet to the room. It was late. He was drunk on the wine from the bridge. He opened the only window in the room and thought about the weird angles that surrounded him in the room. Many francs and necklaces had been lost in an acute corner with a tall dresser jammed into it, creating a triangular void. The truncated rectangle form of the ceiling, chipped yellow paint nearly raining down. An oblong dusty cheap print of a naked lady getting into the bath hung against a green wall. Cool air wafted in through the plastic drapes, which tickled the sides of his face as I got on his knees to see the courtyard.

He lit a cigarette, and it tasted so good immediately, then changed. He threw it down into the courtyard, and the rain put it out shortly after. He was oddly comfortable on his knees on a thin green rug and stayed there for quite a while, his head propped on his hands and elbows resting on the windowsill. Some rain splashed onto his arm from the ledge, mixing with bird shit and cigarettes down below. The rain in Paris was unique to Paris. It didn't bother so much. It seemed to accommodate the ground, and raincoats didn't work as well. It didn't seem to be as wet, and in his mind, a whole different set of properties for water applied when in Paris. It was not necessary to bathe in scalding water. Cool water did just fine. He didn't even bother to test that out. In the middle of the night, he threw up red wine and bread into the sink, and awoke with emptiness and a cold wind.

CHAPTER 19

Croissants and Coffee

All he could think of the next morning was large quantities of croissants and coffee, so he dressed quickly and looked for a café. He found one a few blocks away. In the process of waiting for the waiter, he discovered himself having some Blytheation and wondered why the hell they're called waiters, since he was the one doing the waiting. They should be called ignorers.

He stopped ignoring him after fifteen minutes, and said "Bonjour. Je vous écoute," pen and paper in hand. He ordered the first coffee "Un café au lait, s'il vous plaît, et...un croissant. Merci." He wrote a note to himself and went away. With nothing but time and hunger, it seemed like an eternity. He played with some matches and smoked a cigarette, thinking about his brother.

One night, the parents were on a trip to Australia, and his brother showed him how to inhale a cigarette:

Take a drag

breathe in deeply and hold

Say "My name is [insert your name]" three times over and notice whether or not smoke comes out from the mouth or nares during this test phrase exhale completely

Determine the success of inhalation; a successfully inhaled cigarette should only produce smoke upon the final exhalation, and by deduction, this implies that smoke was indeed trapped in the lungs during the time of speech.

A large café au lait arrived, warm, bubbly milk floats on top, guarding the coffee...the cup teetered on its saucer...came to rest eventually to the touch of Blythe's fingers...

Childhood bubbled up from the bottom: eerie, large bubbles that appeared to be blown to and fro, downwards and downwards deep below the surface by dense, cold currents, thus emerging at the surface irregularly, or not at all. He used to think that bubbles of this sort came from turtles. Then someone said they came from biting turtles. Bubbles came from turtle mouths at the end of long turtle necks that reached out and bit young boys' feet when they weren't too sure of themselves. From then on, he steered clear of bubbles in natural bodies of water.

A cool breeze blew by on the café terrace. Dogs on leashes passed by.

Attic forts, hot like black leather seats in summer, cardboard card tables and beanbag thrones all covered in sap drops and black, crumbling roof tile soot come racing in, unwelcome. Wooden spears, thrown with imagination and whittled by a kitchen knife, killed bears, tigers, and dragons on the lawn. Fences were built not for protection, but for climbing over, since all the space in the world all at once would lead to confusion, and to much abstraction, like a guitarist in the middle of a song, who hears when spoken to but cannot reply, who hears but does not understand because she is in a large field without fences.

A dry croissant appeared before him.

Soccer balls flew higher than planes off his powerful young foot. Eddie Murphy said dirty words, and so did Richard Pryor. *Swedish Erotica* ushered in adolescence. *Pictures of Lily.* He hung pictures and posters of all kinds, of rock bands, of movies, plays, and books, of girls, of athletes, and pictures of his family. He blushed intensely in Mr. Stanzel's science class, and wonders to this day why he crimsoned (when you've blushed as much as Blythe has, you can use the word as a verb for reasons of economy) at the sight of his pointer coming his way. Was he like Kyle when he was young, and wanted to purge this vascular sensitivity, or was he sinister, hateful, and inconsiderate? Could he have known how angry he made Kyle, though he never showed it, and probably never will? Probably.

The sound of a plate falling and breaking emanated from the back of the café. Harsh French words followed.

Basketball fights and swims underwater all the way to the other end. Running in wet shorts. Hot pavement on the back of your legs, wet towels strewn alongside bikes and soda cans. Hot dogs were stolen and mustard sprayed all along clothes like splatter art, and it stained quickly. Smoking pot that Rob stole from his brother and rolled into a large banana joint.

Our first kisses. These were kisses; there is nothing else to say about them. The best kisses, lest we should fall into depression, are always saved for later in life, and even after we've found them, we look forward to yet another, and another, and another, and after that, to ten thousand more. Another kiss never hurts. Fuck those who say kiss and then leave, or kiss and then forget. Kiss and then kiss again. To stop kissing is to stop living. To tease is to live under constant mistrust. To kiss is to trust blindly.

He looked around at the several old men at the café, all of them staring down at something on the table, apparently reading. One had his legs crossed, another extended straight out in front of him. Another man barked into a cell phone, a businessman apparently. That was the first businessman he had seen in Paris, at least as far as he could tell. He wished they would pay attention to him, to authenticate his existence. He felt so unreal, disassociated from his past.

Larger bubbles came more slowly, and these changed the surface of the water for longer. The ivy patch in the front yard, impenetrable to the young eye, save for ball or toy: his legs seemed to pass right through it in the sunlight, and in later years creep through it in the darkness, hoping to sneak back into the house undetected, caught one time by his father exiting the house to go jogging. Coming home smelling of cigarettes and Budweiser, and him smelling of toothpaste, coffee, and *The Wall Street Journal*, both at 4 A.M., now there's contrast and yet smaller ones came forth...brown clay moo-cows, haircuts, shoes, drumsticks, sweatshirts, beds, sheets, and pillowcases, all yellow and stained by now. He always wondered why they were stained the color of piss. T-shirts, underwear, and socks, holes in all by now, some saved in drawers, some used as rags to clean the floor. Magazines, *Playboy*, *Rolling Stone*, and comics, baseball cards, Hardy Boys novels, Stephen King's *It* and *The Stand*, Iron Maiden albums in perfect condition, concert tickets and school awards, all necessary in some way, each and every thought, thing, memory, or fact essential to Kyle's life. Each of them forgotten, misplaced, somewhat erased, or obliterated by the presence of so many other things, physical and emotional.

He lit a Gauloise to try to change his thoughts. It did not help. He took a deep drag, inhaled into his lungs, and said, "My name is Kyle. My name is Kyle. My name is Kyle." A puff of smoke came out of his mouth on the third "Kyle." He blew the rest of the smoke out of his mouth and took a sip of coffee.

As he returned the coffee to its saucer, GI Joe, rocky streams, dead frogs, and fish tanks swirled in his head. Fishtanks and razorblade glass cleaners, charcoal, cotton, flaky food, pumps and fake seaweed, water clarifier and a missing eel. Where the hell did that eel ever go? It swam beneath the pebbles at the bottom of the fish tank the moment it was released. Never a bone, never a scale, never a tooth was found.

All that remained was a vision of it writhing its body into the small pebbles at the bottom of the tank, most likely confounded at the bottom of a new glass universe. Although for all we know, it made it to the ocean. It was never seen again.

Nor were the beer cans that he hid in his Lego chest. Nor were the baseball cards inside a copy of *A Catcher in the Rye*. Nor was his love for his first girlfriend. Nor were the love notes

Dear Ashley, Emily, Lisa, and Kate–he put in a large chest of drawers, in the top drawer, underneath unworn sweaters, spools of thread, underwear, and bras: the inheritances of his sister's occupation of the room before him. Nor were the condoms he stole from the pharmacy and hid in an old wallet in a dress coat pocket in the closet. Those were never found again, either. His mother probably knows the ultimate destination of all these things. Though, to be honest, he has not fully checked on all of them. Some may still be waiting, in hiding, to be put to work unravelling the course of the past, the twists and turns, the blind spots and sudden stops.

Nor will all the things he doesn't remember, or doesn't want to remember...

He stubbed out the cigarette and lit another one. The coffee was nearly full.

One last bubble floated up, twitching rapidly side to side as it rose, promising all the time to degenerate into smaller bubbles, which would fizzle at the top and dissipate, like in soda water. He couldn't stop it…a letter…at the bottom of the drawer…had he put it there? Had someone else found this one letter and saved it while throwing away the rest? He did not recall from where this letter came.

As he took it in again in his mind, the text seemed superimposed on the lined yellow paper. In fact, the paper drops back, assumes a secondary role behind the stark words, as they shift and vibrate and come to life. He lost the difference between word and thought, between sentence and sleep, between page and day, taken in by the lines completely. He ceased to read them. They read him, each and every line read him; they informed him of what he was doing, what he was feeling, and what he should do.

He recalled staring at that yellow page, no date, no salutation, no "Dear Whoever." Just flat text right away:

I think we should spend more time together, away from everyone. I'm sorry about the other day; I had to go. I feel so nervous when I'm with you. You're an amazing person. You make me laugh and feel so happy. That's what I love about you. Let's hang out tomorrow. I'm not doing anything except waiting for you.

He recalled that he had spent some time that same day with a girl: no random girl, his ex-girlfriend. It had been one of their first dates. And yet she denied at the time having written this letter. Not just denied it, adamantly refused any responsibility for it. She clearly had not written it; it was not her typical handwriting. He had always been perplexed by this letter.

It was signed only by a large capital "M" followed by a period, which looked like this:

The strange part was the nature of the "M" itself.

It did not appear to be written. The ink had a lumpy, dry consistency that reminded him of signatures on junk mail. It looked like a stamp, or some sort of insignia.

He had almost forgotten about this "M," which had become a symbol by repeated exposure, and the mere sight of it evoked nightmarish images of international mystery and intrigue, the feeling that someone was looking over you, observing your life from afar and sending you clandestine ideas and suggestions.

What hurt most was the secrecy of the whole thing, as if she avoided putting her name on it like a secret agent, in the name of eternal innocence, avoided ever writing anything down, always memorized every detail: names, places and phone numbers, instructions, plans, and contact networks. He still did not know if the letter was written to him or someone else. He still didn't even know who wrote the damn thing. Nevertheless, the love existed, and it had found an object, no matter who wrote it.

It was so strange that Meghan would not admit to writing the letter, as it had basically crystallized his feelings for her. It sealed the deal, so to speak: they were together in his mind.

And thus the answer is yes, he assumed from the first moment he read it, from the second he laid eyes on the handwriting so typical of a young woman in love, that it was the girl he had met several nights before. The same one who, years later, wrote him letters from Boulder, Colorado. The same one who approached him out of nowhere at a party before they really knew each other said, "Let's be together and not be like everyone else, let's do what makes us happy and just be together." This type of woman easily could have written this letter.

And so the myth was created. A letter had been written, and a recipient had been found. A lover had been either disappointed or deceived, or discovered. So Kyle's life took a long, spiraling path towards possible deception. Truth took hold of everything but him and created a whole separate life, one in which he was the deceived. He had fallen in love with a girl; love had crystallized over a letter.

But he was in France, and his love for her was greater than ever; there was no turning back now, even if his whole life had been a farce. Even if his eyes were gouged out from the beginning, his liver replaced by a carburetor, his intestines a leaky garden hose, his brain a muddled mound of warm butter, his kidneys fishtank filters and his gallbladder a sack of green goo stolen from some crazy chemist even if he was a totally fake human with a history of funk, he was still sure of what he wanted. If the world were totally indifferent and every human desire was to be deflated by the horror of history and death, every passion relegated to the inconsiderate marching of time, the punctilious clicking of a gigantic stampeding clock, he now knew that the only source of comfort and enjoyment for him was in the crystal blue eyes of a girl. Kyle now knew what the meaning of this letter was for him and more broadly. It was that people all over the globe, inside everyone's imagination, ought to take letter writing as the most serious art form that could ever be undertaken. For it chanced to turn certain emotions into impervious forms, whether good or bad, and formed the basis of lifetimes.

Just then, something that resembled rotten mayonnaise landed in his lukewarm coffee, no more than would fit into a thimble. It splashed a bit onto the table and onto the untouched croissant, eating into its buttery outside like warm acid. He scanned the café for laughing children or bitter anti-capitalist Frenchmen with moustaches; after all, he was wearing an Abercrombie & Fitch tee-shirt. He saw neither. He looked to the birds circling overhead.

And yet one last memory came to him. This one is that type of memory that has alluded you for a lifetime. Too many times had he pondered asking his parents for answers, but for too long now the questions had not been asked nor answered, and the unknown, therefore, cemented in time like a hundred-foot rock formation.

Kyle had had a tumultuous period in his childhood. He recalls a medical illness, a shot in his buttcheek for a serious food allergy and near anaphylactic death, and following this, things became cloudy for a few weeks. He recalls spending days and weeks at home without going out for medical monitoring. He spent weeks at home, making up study time from Mrs. Thompson, the school secretary, bringing home assignments. She had been kind. He also used to shovel her driveway for twenty dollars, something that made him happy.

But during this time, he had some extra home time and extra freedom, therefore. He snuck into his parents' bedroom one evening when they had not been home. In his father's drawers, typical memorabilia of military service, antacids, matchbooks, socks, coins, and golf tees, the things a typical middle-aged man would keep in a drawer. He did not look into his mother's things too much, for no particular reason. But there was one locked drawer he knew his mother kept secret from everyone in the family.

She always told the family that was where the most sacred baby pictures, bank statements, and family treasures were kept. She always told the family not to venture there for fear of loss or damage to these precious family keepsakes.

Kyle nervously touched the key, which, although usually not stuck in that drawer, was tantalizingly sitting there, perfectly square and almost begged him to open the drawer.

Kyle froze. He had never even thought about opening that drawer. It was a family respect thing to not do so.

But here he was, a rule-breaking young teenager, about to open the family secret drawer.

Kyle has always thought his memories of the contents of that drawer would be clear and memorable to him. But his mind now shudders to think of what he saw:

Fairly clear family photos of him as a young child, his older brother, and another young girl being cradled in his mother's arms. One or two shots of her. And some baby items like a pacifier and a silver baby rattle, beaten up by years of rattling babies, apparently. Kyle picked it up and strangely smelled the scent of old metal. He held the photo of the young, unknown girl alongside him and his brothers. He had what one can only call the faintest feeling of an unremembered memory, the slightest possible hint of the sound of an infant cry, and a few sparse neurons of his mind went off, then went silent, thoughts that questioned their own existence.

CHAPTER 20

The next morning, Blythe woke up in a grey room in his hotel. His thoughts were highly disorganized, choppy like a shallow ocean in the wind. Yet strong currents ran underneath. He felt that he should not have put himself into such a polarized situation. He could have made decisions to distance himself from the chances of change. Far from the fall, a low position away from the heights of sadness. His head whirred all the while around some inarticulate thought, dimly dancing near the edge of profundity, but with a serene absence of cognition. Yet fluidity comforted him and his joints, which seemed to function sublimely, rolling along like a placid lake, total biological function intact, the physiology working just fine without thought from up top.

Sick with nausea and nail-biting boredom, he decided to walk around. A musty scent had taken over in the lobby. It was a cool, light rain outside. The rain reminded him of searing heat on the beach.

If he could hear his own thoughts, he would probably cover his ears. He walked along in total silence. He concentrated on not even listening to the clicks of the birds in the trees, knocked out of existence the swaying of leaves and the ruffling of plastic in garbage cans and the droning of the cars on the road. He walked right by the scents of cheese shops, no more attractive than a metal pole. Vistas and glorious esplanades he ignored the sight of, training his eyes on the back of his hands and the clean parts of white-gray pavement, not even on the cracks which housed interesting debris, but on the slate-blank flat squares which housed the strength of the street. No thought for sand beneath the bricks. If he saw a brick, he saw nothing, dirt, compressed rocks displaced from history. If he saw a store, he only saw a blurred detail of suffering, a necessity like a heartbeat or a gasp of air, a temporary holdup in the sublimity of supreme nothingness. If he could, he would buy everything, sell it, and burn the money.

The first man he saw, a few blocks from the hotel, was obviously headed to work. He had a confident air. Blythe felt like he had met him before. He queried, in a Kyle tone, "What do you think, a good day?". He responded in English.

"I think today is going to be the best day in a long time."

Taken by surprise, Kyle countered his optimism, "Oh yeah, and why the hell is that?"

"Because this is the first time you've seen this day, and how can you imagine living today any other way without it being exactly like it is today?"

This man, with rawhide boots on his legs and a smirk on his face that says "I had great sex last night and I know what life is all about", spoke like he had known Kyle for his entire life. The minute he saw the coffee stains on his teeth, their cover blown by happy lips, he knew it. He had approached Kyle with just a bit too much confidence, almost as if he'd been asked to check on him. He felt like he was trying to engage with Kyle, and Kyle was quite familiar with the normal feeling of people not wanting to engage with him, so when this chap did so, it felt out of place, like a fishing pole in the Sahara. Once he smelled his perfunctory underarm deodorant, he was sure. Once he saw in his eyes the look of total satisfaction, of happiness, of tired enjoyment, of suffering the enormity of suffering there is to suffer which was present in his eyes and in the arc of his spine, and in his forehead the blissful wrinkles of disagreement and premeditated capitulation, he knew that it was he, that he was the one who had stolen from Blythe all the previously described joys of his life in the form of a single, blond-haired woman who once wrote him love letters.

It was a moment, to say the least. He hung on his last few words with a dizzy gaze at his clean-shaven face. A quick look over: see if there were any more clues as to whom he had spent the past few months near. Instantly, his instincts were to penetrate the lair, to lay quiet, befriend him, and eventually to poke a hole in his web of fake love and thereby release his one and only catch.

But only moments into talking to him, he found himself attracted to this stranger as a person. He had an easiness about him. Relaxation lingered about him like a bee around a warm doughnut. They spoke for a few moments about the weather. Kyle told him he was here to find an old friend, and immediately he took an interest. He could tell this man did not know, despite his eagerness, that the woman he was searching for was probably still laying in this sick man's bed.

He seemed truly jovial and asked Kyle if he would like to grab a coffee at a café. He considered it rather odd that he asked after only a few words between them.

The man said he had a while before he needed to be at work. They sat down at an especially unnoticeable café just down the street from the hotel. Kyle motioned to sit at one of the outside tables, but he did not approve. They walked right into the café, a few tables taken, and chose a comfortable spot near the bar overlooking the street. The table and chairs were simple and refreshing. Kyle was comfortable but intrigued. They ordered, and he asked him why he chose to ask him to coffee.

"Well, my friend, there are certain things I see in people. I happened to have noticed you walk out of your hotel over there, take a few steps, and I thought you looked terribly out of place. Let me...let me tell you a short story, because I thought you looked like I looked, and felt, several years ago. I had an awful case of...food poisoning...well, it was more than food poisoning. At any rate, I was so sick I couldn't make it back to my apartment, only a few blocks from here. So I walked into the lobby of your hotel, the same one, and passed out in a chair. This was very late at night."

"Sounds like you should have been in a hospital."

"I don't disagree, at the time I was unable to. I woke up in the morning to the sound of the telephone ringing. I noticed I had been put to bed in a room, washed, my clothes washed, and there was some food and water left out for me."

"You passed out at the right place. It's a very cheap hotel, but the managers are very nice, I've noticed that."

"Well, I'll get into the details of that hotel some other time. It's enough to say that yes, they are very nice people. They sure took care of me that night. But after that morning, I still felt terrible in the morning. I recall walking out the door, looking much like you do now, unshaven, tired, and worn out. I recall a young guy calling out to me as he drove by, and then he stopped the car in front of the hotel. I was just standing there trying to figure. He said to me, 'Hey, unlucky one, you wanna go have some coffee?'"

Kyle took a sip of the coffee. A wave of repetition went through his head. The man waited for a minute as if he would ask a question, and then continued.

"Of course, I was as confused as you are now. I was at the time as lost and depressed as I had ever been in my life. I did not enjoy anything, girls, alcohol, cigarettes, not even my family. Then this silly man asks me to go have some coffee. It was such a simple invite. He was a total stranger. At the time, I had no idea how influential this one trip to this café would be."

"Were you sitting right there where you are now?"

"No. I was sitting right there." He pointed at him. "Right where you sit now."

"And how long ago was this?"

"Long enough. I don't want to bother you with the details of my life. I didn't stop you from…I didn't decide to do this to destroy your day with my depressing life. In fact, I didn't even decide to do this until a few seconds after I saw you. It was just the expression on your face. Shit, I haven't even thought of those days, of the period in my life when this happened, for a long time. Maybe a few years, I haven't thought of it in years."

"So what made you look at me and decide to…"

"Like I said, it was just your face. A certain expression, maybe the way you put your hand through your hair, or the way you rubbed your eyes. I don't know…"

"You already know more about me than that," I say and bite my lip quickly to punish myself for getting too anxious.

"What do you mean?"

"I told you that I'm...in love with a woman. I think that's where a fair amount of my dissatisfaction comes from."

He laughed a hearty laugh and ordered another coffee.

"Isn't that obvious? I think most men are in love with a woman."

"Sure, but not all men have equal claim."

"Equal claim? Claim to what? Claim to have a woman? She owes you nothing, believe me, despite whatever you think. If you're not at this table right now with this woman that you are in love with, then you must not have been...how do you say...put in your place. This is the first time you are scared to lose something, isn't it?"

Blythe backed up his seat a bit.

"I've lost things before."

"Things that were important to you?"

"Well, I never really know what's important to me..."

"I know, I know, until you lose it. Yes, well, that's obviously never happened to you before. Or maybe you forgot the lesson."

"So what do you do, may I ask you?" he tried to change the subject, feeling that he sensed his interest in his case.

"Well, you can probably guess I don't work for anyone. I'm not looking to impress anyone in this outfit." He points to his dirty pants and yellow tee-shirt, both embedded with labor and sweat. He does not smell like he works at a difficult job, though it is early in the morning, but his clothes look like four o'clock on a hot afternoon. "I'm a mason. I build fireplaces, walls, you know, I work with rocks and put them together in fancy patterns. Sometimes simple patterns, I guess. That's basically the way I make money. But what I really like doing is hanging out with friends and talking."

Kyle tried to act disinterested.

"Sometimes friends are safer than being in relationships. I used to be..."

He got cut off by the waiter. He ordered another coffee and forgot where they left off. The waiter and the man had an exchange, something in fast French that he could not understand.

"Anyways, I think you were saying, oh, I forget where we were."

"You were talking about friends."

"Right. Well, so you work for yourself, independent, I guess you would call it?"

"I haven't worked for anyone since I was old enough to work. I worked with my father for many years. I guess that's working for someone, but he didn't pay me; he just fed me and let me learn about his trade. He was also a mason. But not like me. He only worked for contractors. Big groups of fancy dressers that convinced everyone they were helping them change their social status by building a façade or a marble fireplace. You know, people who install a very expensive kitchen countertop and think that it will change their lives."

He laughed, then their coffee clinked in front of them. It began to feel awkward for Blythe to hate this man. He seemed so jovial, so much different from what he expected at first. It was almost a pleasant thing to sit in a good café and drink coffee with such a person. For a few moments, he even forgot to search for clues to Meghan's whereabouts.

Conversation took a rest; neither of them seemed to mind. He appeared well-rested and content. He noticed his clothes were not that clean, which remained the only sign that he may not have spent time with her. She had always been a fanatic about clean clothes and a "neat" general appearance. Tucked in clothes, short hair, clean shoes and socks. A long time ago, she wore wool sweaters and may have even dreaded her hair at one point. Nowadays, she wears mostly black. The goal of some mothers was to let their children leave the house and attack the world with manners, neatness, propriety, and good sense. Other mothers, Blythe's excluded, chose to leave their children up to their own wiles, with the idea that a kid grows up pretty well all on their own, with a few hits and pokes here and there to aim them in a certain direction. Save for heavy drugs, weapons, forced sex, and suicide, what else out there was really, truly, honestly, going to hurt a kid irreparably?

"So you have your own customers?"

"Ah fuck this word, customers, I don't have customers. I'm not a corporation. There is no panel, no committees, no meetings…" He got a little upset. "Sorry, I didn't mean to get upset. It's just that everyone in America has this idea that everything in the whole universe is taken care of by a corporation. Where does this idea come from? That no single man can make something for himself, or rely on only a few other people to do it? Why is it that an American must have everything made or done for her?"

He thought of several reasons, but decided to tell him: "I guess we're just lazy."

He laughed.

"But how do you make sure you always have work?"

"It's not a problem. I do good work, and I rely on people to tell their friends. That's how it works in this area."

Kyle decided that he was tired of dancing around the subject. He decided to go right for him.

"I see. You know what…let's not talk about work anymore. Or me, for that matter. What about you? Are you…Are you single or with someone, are you married?"

He kicked back in his seat, as if in the middle of an intense interrogation, and the secret box had just been opened. His demeanor became more open, though. The wrinkles around his eyes sharpened as he showed his teeth for the first time.

"I do not have a wife. I have never been married. I do not plan on it. I enjoy my freedom. I enjoy the women that I see. It is a beautiful moment when you first kiss a woman. When you first smell her on your pillow, and you hang on each other in the morning, and lean over for more without the fear of her staying for the rest of your life."

"Hah. But don't you want...anything? Anything that lasts. Don't you want to continue your life, grow a family or have a long life? Don't you have any traditions you want to carry on and pass on?"

He let out a deep, cynical laugh. "What tradition are you speaking of?"

"Whatever your tradition is...whatever it might be that you find important in life and wish to pass on to future beings...beings you care for and think will need it. And by passing it on..."

The waiter passed, and Didier asked for a check. "Listen," he said, "why don't you let me show you something...a good club near Clagencourt that I like. You won't hear about it anywhere else. I have some friends there, and I think you could talk to them. I think these are the people you need...you would like to spend time with. Let's just say that lives go around sometimes, they repeat themselves, and I feel it's just necessary for you to come. Do me a favor. Next week we're having a big event, not a party, more like an organizational affair."

"I don't know. I really should be getting back home. I can't live forever over here without a job."

"Listen. You don't need a job. You only live once. I know that's a cheap reason. Alright, I will make sure that you not only have a good time, but you will appreciate that I invited you. You will not look back after the night and feel like you could have...stayed home...or made money...or done something else."

It was pretty much the fact that he said Blythe would appreciate it. Appreciate it? What a strange way to invite someone. What the hell could he possibly have to show Kyle Blythe at this damn club that would make him appreciate him and his invitation? Appreciation. The only thing he would appreciate would be if he handed over Meghan in a plush car and if he could drive her around Europe to stop only at quiet restaurants, oceans, and sunlit vistas beyond the reaches of their planned trips and beach vacations. The only thing he could ask him for would be experience with her that was contemplative, thought-inspiring, to drink a glass of wine in a park in Paris and smoke a joint right after, and to kiss her right after that. And hope she wasn't sentimental about it. It's not the rejection that's so bad about a kiss sometimes; it's the sentimentality, the appreciation of the kiss that really bothers Blythe. Can't she just ignore the little things, give him some space to be his own strange self, his strange enjoyment of undocumented moments, the escapes from habit, his own perversions of habit and happiness?

The man took a decisive swig at the remains of his coffee and set their departure into motion. He felt that Kyle chose not to take him up on his offer.

"One last chance…"

Blythe hesitated.

"Alright, fine. What the hell. What do we do? Meet you there?"

"Meet me at the hotel, same day, same time tomorrow, in the lobby if you wish, or I'll call up to your room."

"I don't think they even know my name. I'll just meet you outside. What time?"

"How's, uh, 11 o'clock?"

"Okay. Fine. 11 o'clock. Say, what kind of place is this? Does it matter what I wear?"

The man shook his hand.

"Didier Fontaine," he said without a French accent.

"Kyle Blythe. Nice to meet you."

Then he walked away.

The rest of the day melted away like a fade-out at the end of a sad film. He developed a dry cough and a fever, which defervesced with several coffees and a few strolls to Maison

Kaiser, a friendly bakery which had enticed his tongue.

He spent the evening challenging the wait staff to his versions of truth. They listened but consistently walked away with a stiff shoulder. It was Kyle who derived pleasure from hearing himself speak French, certainly not them who enjoyed any sense of enlightenment or a break in the Franco-American cultural rift.

Once back to the hotel, he let in some faint thoughts of Angelina just before slipping into cognitively dissonant sleep. She had once given him a tooth as it fell out of her mouth and into her hand. It was to get a better sense of the uncanny, she said. She did not express any concern about the fact that a tooth had fallen out of her mouth. Though a nervous smile on her face, she simply took the tooth from her hand and put it in his. "From me to you, part of my body," and she laughed. There was no way to understand not understanding; that much was clear.

Blythe met Didier Fontaine at the hotel, and they walked rapidly to the corner of rue de R...and they stood amidst a motley group in front of the basement entryway to a dark, boarded-up four-story building. Garbage, throw-up, panties, condoms, and other debris adorned the sidewalk just outside. A punk scene, crazy scene. No advertisement, no sign or name, as some were let in Blythe caught a glimpse of partially naked women and men clad in leather, plastic, and metal. Blythe was in rather preppy clothes and shoes. He felt out of place just loitering in front of the place, and estranged from himself. He felt like his feet were trying to walk some classy walk that he didn't want to be walking. But he soon realized his feelings were wrong. It was the kind of wrongness that a deer sensed when it ran away from distant headlights in a quiet field.

Some person came up to talk to them as they made their way past the short line out front. Apparently, he knew Didier, although Kyle thought he was about to punch him in the face. He talked in a normal voice, and he didn't look at anything on Kyle except for his face, even as he stepped over people having sex in the entryway, and when he spoke, he did not sound like a punk thug rocker. He was obviously educated, a reader (since he said that the next day for him would be akin to the hangover scene that Slothrop goes through), and did not intend to hurt someone tonight, with his spike-clad arms and fake knife blades on a necklace and angry tone of voice—like Kyle had assumed.

As they floated in a bare-breasted woman with "KISS ON ME" written in red on her breasts "kiss" on her right breast, "on" in the middle, and "me" on her left breast brushed briefly past. It looked like lipstick. A man with a leather helmet on nearly tackles them. Harsh whips and long chains flew around—a poltergeist had infected the objects in the dark red room. A young man fingered a necklace like a rosary. Arms clad with dull metal and black leather flailed at random, sometimes at a perfect trajectory to grab your ear and tug. A barefoot man sat on the floor near the far corner of the room, cross-legged in a black robe, hands intertwined and neck straight, staring straight ahead at the crowd.

Blythe's spirit felt lifted somehow, out of normal misunderstanding into total miscomprehension. He was transplanted into a body, not just foreign, but unnoticed. He would stick around in this body for as long as he wants, he thought to himself, like a vestige of a functioning person. The music was dark and viral, and *All You Need Is Love* by the Beatles crept into his head. Out-of-place drums pierced his delicate ears as arms out of the darkness poked around near his face, his belly, tingling that old, strange feeling that had started long ago. He was uneasy because he couldn't tell the difference between someone who was partying and someone who was on a mission to prove that they could exist at this bar in a moment in time. He sensed that some were here because of a conviction that this place represented something true and beneficial in their lives.

Others were here because they had heard about it and wanted to tell others they'd been there. He felt so far from himself, yet he reached down and put his hands in his pockets like he'd been doing for fifteen years. He was estranged from estrangement.

Blythe wavered next to Didier while he talked to the spiked man. Didier, before the intruder and accomplice, is now his protector in this world where looks cannot determine the safety of a person. In fact, looks could not determine anything, because here perception became irrelevant. He could vaguely try to guess a woman's feelings when she walked down the street in his neighborhood, when a mother ordered a meal for her child, or when a teacher saw a few high school students swear and tease.

Here he was, closed off, totally isolated from normalcy and comprehension. He wanted to be at a restaurant where he understood the contract between waiter and waitress, to wait in line at a movie theatre, or have a bartender ignore him. Here, there were no bartenders, and there was no communication with the people behind the bar. They didn't even seem to pay for drinks. There was a whole different arrangement of forms here. They spoke an entirely new language with lots of different names of drinks, sexual positions, types of marijuana, names of movies and novellas that no one had heard of, nicknames for politicians, terms for money, and expressions of appreciation for art. Kyle was on an alternative West Coast, where the hippies had all died and all the perverts and punks had taken over.

There seemed to be masks on people who were not wearing masks. Then, before his eyes, more gruesome masks morphed on people who were already wearing them. Horrid faces and pretty naked people flew from all directions, some from afar, some without warning. They came faster and faster, sometimes one on top of another. One woman stopped and played with Kyle's shirt. She teased him with a beckoning finger, but he ignored her. She disappeared rapidly, and more people came out of the darkness, clad in yellow, black, red, purple, orange, blue, and pink. No one was wearing white, perhaps the most refined non-color around. Certainly, the most symbolic.

At that moment, symbolism did not matter as much as reality, or any attempt to find reality. Someone grabbed his crotch and vaguely tugged at it as he took the first sip of a warm beer Didier handed to him, then she disappeared, and he really didn't know if she was right next to him or not when he finished drinking the beer out of an oblong object shaped like a shoe.

Suddenly, a strong woman grabbed him by both hands. "I have to show you something," she said to his face in a rush from behind, pressing her warm chest to his back. She ran him through the wet, hot crowd still holding onto both hands.

He was passive; the hands felt so familiar and trustworthy. No one with hands like that could lead Blythe in a bad direction. Believing in statements like these was an offshoot of spending time in places like this, where, in the next moment, after having been dragged through the writhing crowd, passing through black drapes that reeked of grapes, hash, and cinnamon, he was led through a room full of humping mannequins, although some of them a little too real.

The scant light of the previous room became darker. She whispered, "stairs now," right in the ear, so close her breath was hot and high-pitched, a fraction of a second before he stumbled onto the first one, the feet picking up the pace now, running downstairs actually, both her hands clasping his never letting go, passed though doors and down more stairs, down so deep a metamorphosis, people whispering and talking hurriedly, apparently excited about the arrival of one Kyle Blythe. A checkpoint. He heard an exchange, some sort of security. He felt guarded and honored to be here. Blackness enveloped him. They slowed down.

"Smoke" was enunciated by the comfortable female voice and a wet, cigar-sized hash pipe gently placed between his lips. He felt three or four hands grope his stomach after a deep puff of the pipe, and then more, ten or twelve hands investigated his upper portion, head, neck, and shoulders. Not long, they moved on to legs, and before he knew it, his pants were off and the groping stopped. The shirt lifted itself from his upper half, and he blew smoke as it came off, and it comforted him for the last few milliseconds. He opened his eyes slightly wider to try to see what was going on. A glass cup ended up in his hands. "Drink." He took a sip, mango and blueberry hit him hard as the unexpected contents. A hand opened his mouth and poured in a little vodka. "Enjoy," was her last command as she released his hands and walked away and asked someone if she could go. I heard them tell her that she was welcome to stay.

He stood naked in the dark for a few moments, a few brushings of people around, otherwise, hot, damp air and smoke surrounded him. More hands groped and lifted, lifted his left foot and slid on a pair of soft pants, and continued to put a T-shirt on, which smelled freshly washed. A warm glass was handed over, and he took a sip. The lights turned up slightly, and he found himself in a small dingy basement, surrounded by men and women dressed in all black, soft black sweatpants like his, and plain tight-fitting black tee-shirts on all. The warm glass contained hot chocolate, and he took another sip to comfort himself.

As the glass left his lips, a veiled woman approached. Her voice seemed askew, as if thrown. She spoke in a foreign tongue for a few moments, then said in his general direction: "Leaves like jelly singed my feet."

And then she walked away. Heat pummeled his face now with several alcoholic concoctions brewing in his system. The room spun in multiple directions as he labored to orient himself. The crowd condensed, and an intoxicated solitude, a quietness, suddenly fell over the crowd. A mellow light came from one side of the room, and a man in black clothes entered from a curtained doorway onto a makeshift stage. A young woman handed him a microphone. He paced the stage side to side and commenced speaking after he gave the crowd a thorough lookover.

"Folks, rest easy, and be sure you dropped your anger, unhappiness, and desolation at the door. You are here. This is the time and place you have been looking for. Newcomers, I am the

Auctioneer. Don't worry, I ain't selling anything, hell I ain't got anything to sell."

The crowd erupted in laughter.

"But I have been given the wonderful opportunity tonight to attempt to entertain you through the next few moments of your life. Holy shit. I am jumping up and down because I am so fucking happy to see all of you. Holy fucking shit. I'm here to plug happiness pills up your unfulfilled asses. I am happy to be here and even happier to be alive. I am just gonna talk for a few minutes so that you know you're not all totally unique. Many, many of you are indeed unique tonight, for all the amazing reasons that you are unique, random, and just here because you wanted to come. But some of you here tonight are not so unique. Some of you are here for a reason. Some of you have been named as the ones who are here for a reason. Amongst your friends, family, co-workers, lovers, teachers, doctors, and parents...holy shit, now there's a shitty list...there is always at least one of us who knows of our group. And once you know, you'll never forget. Once you've hung out with us for a while, well, let's just say that it's one hell of a way to go through life. In some miraculous way, all of your paths are connected..."

Blythe started feeling dizzy.

He saw Didier streak across the room in a blur. His mind bended figuring out how he negotiated the crowd, the stairs, with all his limbs intact, given the darkness. Moments later, he showed up next to Kyle with equal improbability. He handed him a cocktail, a tall black glass with gin, a single cube of ice, and a splash of tonic water, which was very tasty, bubbly, and heavily loaded with a sedative, he was later told…

CHAPTER 21

Didier and Meghan

It had been a few days since the Moulin Noir. The walls were still hungover practically.

Didier was having a hard time. He had chatted with Lola, and per the terms of his long-term sobriety agreement with her, he had to comply with her wishes, almost no matter how strange or hard they were.

So he waited until a quiet day, a Saturday, when Meghan was not busy and had some downtime. He thought long and hard about what he was to say. Then it just came out, over coffee late one morning, he could not hold it in any longer:

"Meghan, you are a beautiful and deep woman. I have only known you for a few months, but it has been some of the best months of my life. I wish I could plan a life with you, because I have really fallen for you. But at the same time, I feel that I'm living a lie. I feel that your heart does not lie with me. I feel you belong to someone else."

"I'm sorry, Didier."

"Sorry? What do you mean, sorry? You don't have to be sorry."

"No, I mean I should not have led you on."

"You didn't lead me on. I came into your life at a time when I needed someone, and I left myself open so that we fell in together."

"But I should have set boundaries because you're right. My heart is attached to someone else's, and I've been meaning to tell you, it's just hard for me, because I'm not quite ready."

"Ready for what? Marriage? You don't have to get married."

"Not marriage. Part of love is in the attainment of love. Sitting around being in love is pretty boring. Chasing love and thinking of what to do is fun and fresh. I'm just worried love will get stale."

"Meghan, sweetheart, do you think love stories would ever get written, do you think wars would be fought, do you think fortunes would be made, if love were some evanescent thing, evaporating like the dew every morning. Love is more permanent than matter in some ways. Don't block out the love, it is essential to life, and it will not fade if you don't let it."

"I'm just scared. And I'm also sorry. I do think you and I could have had quite a life together."

"Well, true, we could have, but it wouldn't have lasted. I haven't told you everything."

"What do you mean? You shithead. You told me you were in love with me."

"Well, that's true. I'm not saying I'm not in love with you."

"You also have someone else. You should really leave, then, Didier. I don't trust you anymore."

"I'm sorry. I will pack my things. I don't deserve to stay. It was known that you were in love with another, but I did not confide in you what truly lies in my heart, and for that I am forever sorry and embarrassed. But it's not something I really can share."

"What do you mean? There is more to hide."

"No, it's just too hard for me. You see…I am also scared to fully love. I do not want it to fail."

"Didier, as you just said, love is essential. Don't block it. You just told me this!"

"I have to go. I will come back tonight to pack and clean up my things. You are right. You are so right."

Meghan sat down, somewhat defeated, but also seemingly the happiest she had been in a long time. She started thinking and packing her things.

She felt the need to get away. She had been to Arcachon one time and decided she would sit on the beach there for a day or two until she knew what to do with herself.

CHAPTER 22

Ms. Write On Me

Most wouldn't refer to the ensuing day as a typical hangover. Kyle had apparently spent the night at Ms. Write-On-Me's basement apartment on the floor, face down in a pile of vomit. In reality, he didn't feel all that bad. He stumbled upstairs, and right away, it made a difference to be in a nice place. Quiet rooms and faded rugs with a sunlit esplanade of a living room before him, warm British smells of pastries and café au lait. Dustless plants, oxygen in his lungs, breathable air—the real comfort was the air, the breath you could take in this apartment and think it might be a perfectly warm day, in the middle of winter.

He could tell she was American. She had too many clothes around the room, too many pairs of jeans, and too much food in the refrigerator that he threw up in, to be from anywhere else. He didn't even think of the fact that she had written something in English on her chest. That probably tipped the proverbial balance towards the American side in his head before he even heard her speak. He certainly did not remember hearing her speak the night before, yet assumed at some point she spoke the words "You're sleeping here" or some other derivative of similar value.

She had heard him wake and appear from around the corner.

"Sorry about the drugs, it's the kindest way they've come up with, to my knowledge." She paused as she appeared from around the corner. He vaguely considered trying to ask her what happened overnight, but realized he was probably better off not knowing.

"So how are you feeling?" she asked from behind as she pointed him the way to the bathroom to wash his face in a cold Parisian sink.

"Never felt better...can't you tell..." he stopped as he looked back at her with a dripping face, the cold water waking him now.

"You didn't, d'accord," she said emphatically.

"Didn't what?" After she gave him one of those don't make me say what I am thinking " looks, she motioned to her breasts through her shirt. He could vaguely read the words through the shirt; it must not have been lipstick.

"It's temporary, okay? I'm an actress in a semi-pornographic play, and this is a temporary tattoo. I'm not some kind of fuckup pervert chick, please don't treat me as such, got it?"

"Damn, ok," he said, and she laughed. "How did you get me here?" For the first time, he noticed the honest wrinkles framing her eyes.

"I was sitting behind you, and I offered to take you home. The next thing I knew, we were in a taxi together. You told me the whole story of why you are in Paris, and then halfway through telling me about the beach and how you found her, you passed out on my shoulder...I think you were crying...so I thought you could use someone to take care of you for the night." She looked down at the ground.

"Interesting. Could you fill me in on why I'm here, because to be honest with you, I think I'm losing my...my...?"

"Your mind or your wallet? Here's your wallet. You tried to give it to the cab driver last night." She handed him his wallet casually.

"I guess I must have thought he needed one." He wanted to know more about what had happened; maybe in his stupor, he revealed something to her that he didn't know about himself. "Did I say, do, anything else worth knowing about? Did I tell you much?"

"Well, it was jumbled, but pretty clear that you're here to kill the man that your ex-girlfriend, what's her name, something with an 'M'?"

"I hope you're joking."

"What, she's your wife, not your ex-girlfriend?"

"No, she is my ex-girlfriend. I was never married to her." He smiled momentarily at the thought of M. and him getting married in the near future.

"But I'm not going to kill the guy. I mean, sure, I'd like to see his intestines separated from his body and hot acid poured down his throat, but I would never kill him. That's not why I'm here." His head pounded like never before.

"Well, I sure thought you were serious last night. So I looked up this book this morning on the internet: *How To Kill Your Lover's Lover and Get Away With It.*"

"There's really a book with that title out there?"

"Are you really as gullible as you look?"

"I guess so...how gullible do I look?"

"As gullible as a fish." She walked away toward the kitchen.

He contemplated her statement for a moment and mentally abandoned it when he heard her open the refrigerator and scream. He tried to change the subject instantly.

"Um, did we do anything sexual last night?"

"What do you think?" she answered with her hands clasped over her mouth. "Do you think you marinated the contents of my fridge here in puke and then serenaded me with regurgitated crème brulée? There was about as much sex going on here last night as there was in my grandma's panties after she went on diapers."

"I'm sorry. I didn't mean to make a joke. It's just that everything seems kind of funny to me in the morning."

"Forget about it. It's not important. What is important is what is your name? I still don't know."

"Most people call me Kyle."

"Well, Kyle, we've got some cleaning to do. Let's get to it before the day's over."

"I'm not too concerned about this day being over too soon."

"Why not? It's beautiful out there. And you're in Paris, for chrissake. I don't even know you, but it seems like you're a fun-loving guy, up for underground parties and the like, and definitely comfortable with strangers. Let's have at Paris."

"I think I'm too depressed to stay in Paris. It fit my life before, a few days ago…what day is it? I think it's too late. I lost her to normalcy. I lost her to a real man in Paris, a man who knows how to love a woman. I'm gonna catch a flight home after I clean up your fridge, of course. Sorry about that."

She could have made it easy for him. She could have simply said one thing to make him stay, the least bit of effort, a little bit of sympathy, one little pat on the back. But she didn't. She just giggled a bit as he revealed his pathetic state of mind. So she forced him to leave out of self-pity.

"What do other people call you?"

"What?"

"You said most people…"

"Oh, a nickname." He hesitated.

"Well..."

"Blythe."

As he was walking out of her apartment, however, she yelled from the top floor of the building:

"Let's go to dinner...somewhere...before you leave. You told me too much to just leave. I have to tell you what I think."

She was so high up that he couldn't remember how he got up that high. Nor did he recall descending stairs that far down.

He yelled back, trying to attain her heights, somewhat muted, and shielded his eye as she retucked herself. "I'm sorry. I'd really love to. But I really have to go. I'll remember you. Thanks for taking care of me."

"Just go find her, you weirdo. She'll have you if you tell her everything and how you came here. Just trust me, it'll work out."

He smiled and waved. She smiled back and closed her window.

He walked away from her apartment—one formerly sullied fridge spotless—and enjoyed a few hours of the worst feelings he had ever felt. He stumbled around the streets of the Latin Quarter; a jazz club mocked him with entry fees; café after café offered no more than a solitary table and a waiter's rude shrug; fromageries emitted putrid fungal odors, though smelling as he did, he had no right to label anything putrid in absolute terms.

The eager fruit and vegetable stand owners erected their metal poles and canopy covers, and they made him feel deviant. Water flowed quickly in the gutters along rue Raspail. Hausmann had done a nice job on the streets of Paris, broad, diffuse round corners, no sharpness and hardness, and claustrophobia and metropolitan sludge like New York City. At least you feel good in the morning in a city like Paris. It seemed easier to be sleepless and melancholy, more like it's the thing to do, a good way to be on any given morning, the only thought in his head being good cheap food and somewhere warm to sit and enjoy looking at people. People, no matter what kind, are often the most comfortable souls around. Take a clown, a baker, an athlete, anyone who can exist beside another person and treat them like an equal, even a nobody like Kyle, for he really is nothing. He is not a professional, nor a philosopher, nor even a judge. He doesn't work for money at the moment, doesn't own anything, except for a few pairs of clothes, a smelly couch, and a dog leash. Even those notable things, he didn't consider property, just coincidental existence.

Near dark, he purchased a few packs of Gauloises and a cup of coffee. The barman did not understand his French very well when he asked him to hold the bird shit.

He was so dark and viral, infected, sick really, with the first pack of empty cigarettes in his hand, a crumpled-up newspaper feeling like an old, bitter manuscript in his back pocket, and a leaky cup of coffee on a Jardin de Luxembourg bench. He was a void, a walking lungs and stomach with nothing but old coffee and sick cigarette tar. He needed to change these seemingly orchestrated emotions soon, or they would scar.

He pondered for a moment, the sun still well hidden behind a thick patch of clouds, how she leaned out the window and asked him to go to dinner. It was such an earnest invite. It seemed like a redeemed life form where he was now...cold, hungry, and lonely. He had forgotten to ask her name, but he at least remembered her apartment location. He had no way to get back to Didier, but he could go through her.

Gumption hit him hard as he sat on the bench. If only he hadn't been so hungover. Perhaps she knew Didier. He had the feeling that everyone at that party sort of knew each other. Even if she did not know him, perhaps she could show him back to the Moulin Noir so

he could use the last moments in Paris for one
last try.

CHAPTER 23

The next day, the weather started to change as he headed toward her apartment. It had been sunny, and he could tell it was changing seasons since it was cold in the sun. He walked faster and faster to keep himself warm. He stopped once and tightened up his clothes around the fringes and lit a cigarette. The first drag tasted like rebellion since it was cold again, and they taste different in the cold. He was ready for the smell of them to linger on his hands longer. He was ready for dull red cheeks and unfulfilling sunlight. His mind tried to tell itself that it would be best to spend this wintertime alone, in New York, and enrich itself with the wonders of loneliness and discomfort, with downtrodden glances at cold bums and second guesses near liquor shops.

Coffee suffices to replace the warmth of motion and vibration that cold leaves in its wake. Cold slows life down a little, preserves it, and forces one to cherish the rare silent spaces of the city.

Boulevard St. Michel, rue St. Jacques, Place de la Madeleine, they're all the same in Paris, as long as you're wearing your own pants, shoes, you know, or a shirt with a history. Blythe had not left himself in New York, that's for certain. His dreariness climbed back into the pilot's seat for a few minutes. He eyed a woman, dressed to the nines in elegant French style, her eyes so cold it brought a shudder to his chest. The street he stared down at was so brazen and cold. Standoffish cities like Paris were not welcome to the likes of Blythe.

As he passed strangers they turned up their collars and pull their lovers closer to them. Park benches were empty. Sunlight faded already, and Blythe realized he has been walking for hours. He hadn't really been paying attention to where he was going. The general direction seemed right to him, but he was not sure. Nothing was right now. The sidewalk and its imperfect joints and cracks in buildings, which usually denote character and age, showed structural weakness and neglect. His belt was too tight, and his pants were too long and too large around the waist. He peeked down at the familiar backs of his hands and saw cold, shaky fingers, decrepit and dry.

He walked back to her apartment and stepped over the green entryway into the corridor. He started up the stairs, his back hunched like an old man's. He tried to straighten it, but found himself exhausted. He stopped halfway up to catch his breath. Frustrated with his decision to come here, he lit a cigarette. He felt like a child running to his mother because he knows of no other source of consolation in the universe.

He got to the top of the landing and put out the cigarette on the floor. He took a look across the hall at the door that he barely recognized. With deliberate steps, he made his way to her door. His hand shook a little as he knocked three times and immediately pressed an ear to the door to wait for a sign of movement from within. But he heard nothing.

He leaned against the railing just outside, and stared at the dark brown wood and wondered how hard it was. It is plain, with no details other than the simple four-panel frame on the outside. The doorknob was not round. The hinges were not visible.

As he reached out to knock again, it opened quickly. He wasn't quite ready to understand…

…how Lola had ended up at "WRITE – ON – ME" girl's apartment in the middle of Paris. She wore the same *RED SWEATER* as in New York. But the smell of good marijuana and heavy cigarette smoke brought him back as well. As he walked in uninvited like a zombie, he heard her talking about Harlem. Her unpacked bag lay in the corner of the room, and his imagination superimposes a stylized capital "M" followed by a period on the hard plastic of her suitcase. She is sitting beside a few people he did not recognize. They are red-faced and stoned.

"I think I know you," he blurted out immediately.

"Of course, you know me, you're the roommate. And I'm Lola." She stood up awkwardly and swept her hands open as if unveiling a large statue.

"Everyone, meet the crazy scientist roommate, apparently in from New York and roaming around Paris. And he's definitely been living it up," she said with a querulous smile.

He was taken aback. "That's a flattering description, thank you."

The odd rejoinder allows him sufficient time to look over the room quickly. A bunch of people he did not recognize were all sitting around a large open suitcase with a few random items inside.

He wondered why she thought he had been "living it up," and quit wondering when he caught an image of me in a window on the far side of the room. Rather quickly he changed his mind about something he thought about a long time ago...an idea about compassion for those who look like they have not been happy for a long time...for a person sitting on a cold dirty street with oversized shoes, a can of beer, and second-hand cigarette butts collected in an old hat...looking like they have vomited out all their passion and energy onto the street for public display, whether or not they are conscious of it...

"Well, it suits you well. You're not only a scientist, you're an explorer if I remember correctly?"

He tried to grab another look at her suitcase. There were people lying all over the floor, and he couldn't make it over to get a better angle.

"I don't know about an explorer. Sure, I climb on rocks sometimes, but not much more than that."

"Let's just say that I wasn't talking about anything physical. But never mind that nonsense. Michel, can you clear some room for Kyle here?"

A man named Michel piles up all the clothes on top of the suitcase and pushes it out of the room, out of sight.

"What brings you to Paris?"

He high-stepped into the lazy crowd and sat down on a deep red couch. He couldn't help but rub his greasy forehead and put his hand through my hair. He attempted to answer her but only produced a long sigh.

"Ah, so it's a woman," she intones.

He looked up at her and smiled. The others in the room disperse into their own conversations, collectively aware of the oddly personal exchange.

"How did you guess that? Do I have suffering branded on my forehead?"

"No…but it's in your eyes." She took a long drag on a joint, threw it in an ashtray, and lit up a cigarette. She blew it in his face on the first drag.

"My eyes, huh…what else do you see there, oh seer?"

"Nothing else. It's pretty simple. What I see in your eyes makes it quite clear."

She blew out more smoke like a steam vent. She seemed to vibrate, and for a moment, it tickled the hairs on my arms. He started to feel uncomfortable talking in front of the other people, especially since she hit a bull's-eye.

"How can you tell that?" I posed to her.

At this point in the conversation, she began to quit paying attention to him. I was a bumblebee, and she was a honey-ham sandwich. She was on a salary, and he just went on unemployment.

"Wait…wait a minute…could you not abandon me for a minute…" he pleaded. She smiled coldly as she fixed her attention on me. Now she was distant.

"Indeed, I have been doing a lot of exploring lately…and I'm curious what you were talking about…you…you seem to know a fair amount about me. I mean, I'm tired, but I'm not too proud to show that I need some…help."

"Have you ever been to a psychic? You've never seen a psychic, have you? You've never even had to deal with feelings of disappointment. Am I right?"

She paused to relieve her cigarette of its cumbersome ash.

"I'll tell you what you should do. Go see a tarot card reader," she said as she pointed her finger with the cigarette in the lead. "You know, one of those ladies who live in neon-light-lined basement apartments near bridges in New York. The type of store you would usually never enter and probably scoff at? Am I right? Have you scoffed before?"

"Well, not exactly scoffed, but you're right, I've never even thought of…"

"I went to see one once. She told me everything. She told me everything exactly like I wanted to hear it. And you know what, I asked her how the hell she knew all this stuff about me."

"You can't reveal the magician's secrets."

"Yeah, I know all that. Anyway, I told her I was not going to leave her shop…this poor lady, she had no idea how strange I can be…Anyways, I told her I wouldn't leave the establishment until she told me how she knew all this crap about me."

"And what did she tell you?"

"Nothing at first."

"What did you do?"

"I stayed."

"How long?"

"A few hours."

"Then what did she tell you?"

She paused to smoke.

"She said sex and love."

She didn't seem like she was going to continue. We waited…

"That's all the tarot card readers need to blabber about to make you and me, and all you shitheads too, wonder. Wonder, that's it. Wonder if there is some way for people like the tarot card reader to see into our futures and to read the lines on our hands. All it takes is a little latent unhappiness, a glimpse of loneliness, a hint of a seeker's curiosity, a tinge of the broken heart or the sexless soul ...hell she said a few sparks of electricity on those silly globes...you know the electric orbs, it looks like there's little tiny lightning bolts emanating from the center and it's fun to touch them...well that's only an operational definition..."

Chuckles from the crowd.

"Anyways, she says that just a little spark from one of those coupled with promises of sex and love is enough to get most people's curiosity whipped up into a frenzy so orgasmic that they'll get down on their knees...froth at the mouth...promise sexual favors, money, stock options, she really said someone offered her stock options...just to get the most minute detail about the future. She said it's really not even necessary to predict something consequential in a person's life. Unhappy people can't deal very well with large changes, despite their unhappiness with their current situation. Only the ones that seem mostly happy does she ensnare with some really important or catastrophic predictions."

"Why the happy ones?" he asked.

"Because think about yourself, scientist. If your objective ass was silly enough to walk into a psychic's lair at this moment, you'd be on your knees praying for the predictions so fast that your...your...Ahh, I don't know what the hell you put in your own colorful idiom. You'd want to hear that anything will change, but you'd be afraid."

"Afraid of what, of being happy?"

"No, being more depressed."

"That's not possible."

"Come on, scientist, you're depressed, but you're not totally finished."

"If I get lower than I feel right now..."

"It can always be worse. You could look in the mirror one day and decide that you hate yourself completely for the rest of your life. I praise myself every day I wake up and my all-encompassing organ up there at the top of my head as well, since it's managed to keep a good balance of chemicals in my head."

"Don't give your brain too much credit."

"Why not? If you took my brain out of my head, you would be so amazed. Think where this thing came from...billions of years...a primordial brew...some heat and light...and over millions of years…and like a millisecond frame in a feature film, the ultimate unhappiness machine appears in the last few scenes."

"Well, as I was saying, you're pumping nicotine, marijuana, alcohol, and other alterations to your chemical container of a body all the time. I'm not saying it's bad. But let's not exaggerate how good our life is here. Hell, caffeine is to me what acorns are to neurotic squirrels."

"Well, a lame metaphor doesn't explain your example. You could have…"

"Alright, a squirrel searches and searches and plants acorns all over the place," I cut her off. "Can a squirrel possible be happy and content if she is always, continually, and perpetually putting away future assurance of technical happiness…can any one moment be that good if always, every day, we are planning for more moments…hoping for the perfect moment…one that will be so incredibly sublime that it will change the rest of our life…and all other moments will be deeper, ecstatic, more profound, everlasting?"

"Your life is complicated," comes from an unknown.

He was dumbfounded, demoted in spirit.

"I completely agree. We are forever alienated from happiness by definition. Bliss is a comet." She pauses. "Sublimity is instability."

"I like that, a comet," he added.

"Alright, Ptolemy, come back down and smoke this joint," the unknown says, handing him a joint. He took a long puff, and it eased his tense shoulders for a moment.

"A comet comes back from time to time."

He relaxed around the others in the room for the first time since he had happened upon these friendly people.

A few deep breaths later, the crows dispersed, some food got delivered at the front door, and people started eating in the background. His lungs heavy with warm viscous fluid, eyelids denser than normal, stomach empty, and body warm, he fell asleep on a quiet couch in the corner of the room to the sound of a friendly crowd of people eating.

CHAPTER 24

Lola in Paris

He thought he would just check Meghan's apartment one last time before he tried to find Mrs. W-O-M's place again. He sprinted up the steps and found her door.

"She went to Arcachon?"

"Oui. Arcachon. She left a few days ago." A young guy who spoke English with a French accent said while locking up the apartment next door. He looked friendly, so Kyle asked him if she was home. He said she went away for the weekend, to the beach or somewhere like that.

"She took the train, I think," he said with a quizzical look. "She was telling me how she's going to finish some trashy romance novel on the way down there."

"Do you know how long?"

"Just a few days, I think. She didn't say, but I do have plans with her on Friday. So I assume she'll be back by then." He smiled as he finished locking his door.

"Do you know what size her bra is?" he mumbled under his breath, old feelings creeping in.

"Excuse me?"

He did not hear what he had said.

"Never mind. Thanks for your help."

He waited by the door until he went down the old, round stairs. He knocked anyway, just to make sure she wasn't there. There was no answer, and he said "merde" aloud to himself. An old woman cracked open the door on the other side of the hallway. She whispered something in French and then closed the door abruptly. A few doors down, another opened, a young boy peered out, and then a large hand shut the door gently. Some security around this place. In New York, you could scream outside someone's apartment, and no one even opens their door. Here, one knock starts the whole place crawling.

He leaned back on the railing a few paces from the curious old woman's door. All he could think to do was smoke a cigarette. The Gauloise burned bluish as he took a few drags. The smoke blew down the hall past the old woman's door. It startled him when the door opened slowly, the chain still fastened.

"You cannot smoke over there. Allez-vous-en."

"Désolé," I say to her.

"Allez-vous-en."

"Excuse me, madame, can you please tell me where Arcachon is?"

"Arcachon? Près de la côte. Une grande montagne de sable. C'est interdit de fumer ici. Allez-vous-en."

She slammed the door.

"Merci, madame," he addressed her door. Her shoes' shadows remained present just underneath the wide bottom gap.

He continued to smoke for a few moments. On his third drag, he heard her footsteps moving away from the door. Short, slow, dragging footsteps. He felt bad for the old woman, so he put out a frustrated cigarette on the bottom of his shoe and carried it down the stairs to the street. An old man's bald head blocked the way out. He bowed down near the entryway to the apartment, breathing heavily over a metal cane. He dropped the cigarette and approached his arm with friendly help to see if he wanted help. Before he said anything, he mumbled "Merci monsieur, vous êtes très gentile" through shaky lips, freshly greased with food, and grabbed onto Kyle's arm. He negotiated the small steps leading into the courtyard while Kyle smiled at him.

He mumbled something else quite incomprehensible as he made his way up the stairs. Two flights up, he stopped for a moment. Then continued. Kyle watched him and made sure he would not fall. Strangely, they reached the top step, and he shuffled his way to Meghan's door and knocked three times.

"Excusez-moi, monsieur, je crois..." he started, but the old woman whipped her door open and interrupted.

"Ici, idiot." She clapped her hands twice as a stimulus for her husband. She almost drove them both crazy.

The old man turned abruptly and smiled at her. She did not look at either of them. He walked to her without assistance, his gait faster than before, his back and neck straighter, and his forehead less wrinkled. They disappeared into their apartment with a swiftly shut door. That made Kyle very content. If he hadn't run into this old man, he most likely would have gone straight to the airport and caught a plane for home. Instead, he made a phone call, exchanged the return ticket for an open-ended one, and rented a car.

CHAPTER 25

Arcachon never sounded like a French name, he thought. He only knew that it lies on the Western coast near Bordeaux, a few hour drive from Paris. He said it several times in succession aloud to himself in the white rented Volkswagen. It was not an easy pronunciation. It leaves the jaw kind of tired after saying it a few times. It felt good to drive in France, at least at this point, when he was so unsure of what he was going to do when he got to Arcachon.

He smoked continuously. With the window open and the wind gentle, he felt healthy and let his arm hang out the window. The sun shone off the blonde hair on his arm and nearly blinded him.

He turned off the radio that was babbling in fast French. And he hummed a tune, he thought it was Jimi Hendrix, and he remembered humming it on the bus in New York City. That's where he had just come from. And yet here he was, in France, on the highway, in a car pushing the gas pedal down to the floor which releases bursts of gasoline into a piston, igniting by way of electricity, and pushing outward on the piston, which got translated into torque and eventually into a torque applied by the axle on the tires, and therefore a frictional force on the road by the tires, which results in forward motion. Anyways, he was in France, he was driving. He was driving to Arcachon. He said it aloud a few times: "Arcachon. Arcachon." Briefly, he compared the word to the American prison of lore, the hyperbolic dungeon and perpetual torture chamber, Alcatraz. He said that aloud as well: "Alcatraz." Then he said:

"Arcachon. I am going to Arcachon." He was alone in the car, and with the window open, no one could really hear him. So he started yelling.

"I am going to Arcachon.

I *am* going to Arcachon."

Then he started changing the accent to different words, still saying as loud as he could without breathing too heavily.

"I am going to Arcachon.

I am going to Arcachon.

I am going to Arcachon.

I am going to Arcachon.

I am going to Arcachon."

Then he started yelling it as loudly as he could. It hurts his throat, but he kept saying it. The word Arcachon sounded Asian when he yelled it. "Arcachon," he lost the French pronunciation. "Arcachon!" He even forgot what it was for a minute, whether it was a word or a place.

"I am going to Arcachon! I...I am going to Arcachon."

Not loud enough. The window was wide open.

"I am going to Arcachon."

As I said the last time, he looked to his side to see a woman laughing at him as she drove. He laughed with her and waved, his mouth emitting an unheard "bonjour." She pressed down her accelerator and propelled her car forward with a higher rate of fuel injection than his. He did not try to catch up to her. He didn't care. He only cared about getting to Arcachon.

He asked himself what he would do when he got there. Well, if he were in Arcachon, and the beach was still there as that guy told him outside her apartment, he would be on the beach. The beach. He didn't have any shorts to wear. He was wearing pants and sneakers only. He would be much more comfortable on the beach in sandals and shorts. He thought he could probably get some near Arcachon.

Sand began to appear on the fringes of the highway, where the road melts into the shoulder. Signs became further and further apart. He had not yet seen one for Arcachon, though. He had been on the road for two hours, and he figured it should be coming any time soon.

He realized that my stomach was aching. He was hungry. He couldn't really tell what he was hungry for, and he instantly wondered if French highways harbor those wonderful American mass-marketed contrivances that offer hopes of coronary disease and love handles in one small brown "Upsized ©," recycled, grease-lined, advertisement-riddled bag. Goddamnit, he couldn't even drive somewhere he had never been before, as far away as he had ever been from American consumption, and still he thought of it. Still, the big, brilliantly colored billboards with dollar signs and offers of happiness. Still, he consumes.

He eyed a sign for Arcachon: 30 kilometres. His stomach stopped being hungry and commenced to churn out large quantities of nervousness, the stuff of anticipation and excitement, the stuff of anxiousness and desire, the stuff of creation and destruction, the stuff of having fun and feeling depressed, the stuff of expression and nothingness, the stuff of future and past. He felt like a real person for the first time in a while, and he set the odometer to zero.

Two kilometers later, he lit a cigarette and raised the window just high enough so that the ashes got sucked out for the most part.

At seven kilometers, he lit another one to ease the boiling stomach. His palms began to sweat, and he adjusted myself in the seat.

At 15 kilometers, he checked the radio, did the math in his head. Halfway there. The stomach was twice as productive. So he figured my gastrointestinal discomfort was inversely proportional to how far away he was from Arcachon. Maybe when he gets there, I will have full-blown lesions on my stomach lining, or a perforation for his luck. He felt as if he was giving up a sickness that had somehow made him unhappy for a long time. It's as if he was nervous to see if happiness is really as good as it sounds. If it's not, well, that just sucks.

At 19 kilometers, he put the cigarette out and turned off the radio. He needs a clear head and smoke-free air to breathe deeply. He might even quit; it was not healthy to smoke, and he knew it in his heart.

He came to the exit for Arcachon, and he pronounced the word out loud for the last time, definitively, as if he'd won it as a prize. A small exit road veered off to the right and came immediately to a right turn with a small brown sign pointing to the right. "To Arcachon."

As he made the turn, his foot fell off the accelerator, gas momentarily ceased to enter the engine, and the car slowed; the dunes of Arcachon finally came into view. Mountainous female valleys built of smallness are the only thing now lying between him and love and the ocean. On the one side, Kyle is lonely and smelly. On the other hand: beauty, originality, existence.

CHAPTER 26

A short black paved pathway twisted up the dune to the left, lined by table after table of sunglasses, home-made petit djembes, sun lotion, cheap books, beach mats, and an extensive selection of postcards for sale. This was a tourist trap. He is surprised she has come here. She hates tourist traps.

The path yielded to sand as he climbed higher, the grade eliciting a bit of heavy breathing and plenty of sweat by the time he reached halfway, at which point there appeared informal eating spots and bathrooms. He took off his shoes, just like everyone else had done in the vicinity: older women with children draped around them and chests barely covered under sagging shirts tied in the back in wet knots. His white socks and Nikes come off easily, and the hot sand welcomes his feet to the beach.

He wiped the sweat from his forehead and realized that he had been smiling since the moment he got out of the car. A few pounds of sweat later, the hill breaks and a large ocean extended before me. He looked left and right and told myself that he would find her on the left, for no good reason. He veered towards the left of the horizon, thinking that there was probably a small chance that she was lying on the beach directly in front of him, bathed in suntan lotion and hair tied up in the back, hopefully wishing he had put it on her back, hopefully thinking of them being back together.

He walked quickly down the beach as much as possible with sand walking, the sand squeaking as he stepped on it. The sand is so hot that he heads directly for the water to cool his feet. He stepped on hordes of seashells before he reached the foam. The sand was a bit cooler here. He reached water on its way in and said "ah" aloud as it rushed over his toes and up his ankles. He stopped before the water got his shorts wet and imagined Meghan next to him, both of us ankle deep in wet sand.

He stared at the ocean. This was the first time he had stopped moving for the whole day. That had made him feel fatigued. His legs felt weak. The ocean rippled, waves toppled and rolled in front of him; it threatens to upheave, to boil, to drown, to suffocate, to topple, to sink, to swallow, to crush. And yet it also promises to rejuvenate, to flatten, to equilibrate, to oxygenate, to breathe, to support, to float, to spit, to froth, and to expand. It continually decomposes and regenerates. It recedes and it advances. It shines and it darkens. It lies still, and it roars. It breaks and it polishes. It takes from us and it brings us so much happiness.

At this moment, he wanted to encase the entire ocean and himself, the beach, and feelings in plastic wrap, thick industrial-strength plastic wrap that resisted tearing on the sharp ocean coral dredged onto the beach. He wanted to preserve this exact concert of feelings: a stiff enough wind to make waves show their instability and to cool my hot skin, a taste of salt in the air, sand wet enough to cool hot feet but dry enough to squeak just a few meters away and to provide support to walk quickly on, clear water covering his ankles then receding back into the ocean pulling his legs to make him feel invited.

Yet the ocean was not jealous. Kyle exited the ocean and lay near it and dried himself in the sun. That is what he expected her to be doing: lying on her stomach, her head on her hands with her hair tossed to one side. Maybe she had been reading a book, or perhaps she had brought nothing to the beach except for a towel or a shirt. Perhaps she was considering sleeping through the red sun images and tumbling saltwater noise, punctuated only by an occasional laugh or shout, each one hinting of either fun or danger, or marred as a haphazard passerby kicks up sand into a tired pink face with a dragging foot. But then sometimes this passes by without a trace of disruption, welcome grains of sand joining others already stuck on the face with salt water and sweaty suntan lotion, the old grains indistinguishable from those propelled by inconsideration and hurry.

He thought about running into the water to rinse off the sweat and sand. Whatever she was doing at this moment, he could not see her. He could not find her. He looked left and right, high and low, near the water and far from it, under umbrellas and on top of towels; he looked at clothed people and at naked people. He looks at men as well, to see if maybe he could pick out the one man who may be spending time with her. Maybe he was watching her things or waiting for her to come back from a cool swim in the ocean. What an asshole if he's on the beach waiting for her; for he has no idea how she looks when she swims, how her hair slicks back and her eyelashes stick together. How she wrings the water out of her hair and how her hands feel when wet when they rub your back.

He has no idea what she laughs like in the water. He does not know that she likes to kiss underwater, that she likes to jump on your back and try to drown you, that she gets cold quite easily in the water, even though she is a strong swimmer. He really must have no idea what it's like being with her.

What it's like being with her...

What is it like not being with her? That Kyle has come to know well in the past few months...years...the past few years that he has lived. It is this anticlimactic moment, though, in which he sees everything in total clarity, all the clarities there are to see in the world. Not a grain of sand escaped his view. A sudden flame rendered the congealed thoughts—decisions, impetuous commitments, constraints, in sum, all his diets of intellect—fluid in his mind. What had he been doing all this time? The search had become desperate, and in desperation, he would do nothing but damage. He decided that what he desired out of life—the girl, obviously—could only be found by an act of bravery.

Finally, I leaned towards the left, his feet lifting out of the sand and producing a sharp sucking sound. He walked down the beach, hot on the top and cold below. He continued to scan the beach for any sign.

CHAPTER 27

Angelina

Angelina pondered the density of a ripe tomato as her double-D© serrated Cutco knife sliced into it, beads of pink juice collecting as the blade exited. She sliced it down the middle, absent symmetry worry, but achieved near-perfect symmetry. She was unhappy with her slice, though. She took one of the halves and cut it at an angle to produce something a little more interesting, something that she had seen fewer times in her life. Still unhappy, she pulled another tomato off the vine, leaving the rest in a plastic bag. This time, she decided to leave part of the green stem attached, and again, she severed the skin of the tomato, this time at random, with disregard for angle or linearity. She stepped back and looked at the two severed tomato halves, then forward again and put the knife down next to the wooden cutting board. A few wet tomato seeds lie near the tomato that caught her attention. She grabbed her paints and began mixing some colors.

The phone rang quietly, and she had red paint on her hands. She rinsed them off quickly and did the rest with a paper towel as she headed for the phone. Her friend Mirabelle was on the other line, and she asked Angelina if she could come over for a few hours to watch TV, to get away from the books, she says. Angelina was ecstatic. She screamed at her to get over it as soon as possible and hung up immediately.

For some reason, after the quick call, she thought about how she used to accuse herself of focusing on art for the wrong reasons. She used to think that painting or sculpting or writing was an expression of something in her head that shouldn't be there, a desire to expose her inner feelings to others, to show others that she was miserable at some points, that she was nervous, anxious, tense, hateful, embarrassed, depressed, energetic, manic, mad. She had hidden these feelings, these perceptions, for a long time while she tried to find a job, tried to find a person to live with, tried to make herself feel good in a world of fast computers that can help people make money to buy expensive cars.

She concentrated on the tomatoes. The red paint, accentuated by green, looked too red to her, so she threw a tinge of purple in it and a smear of yellow. Nope, that was not it. She tried and tried to recreate something that appeared so simple at first glance. But Mirabelle arrived and was only slightly annoyed when Angelina asked her about coloration.

"Well, there are usually just a few molecules that are coded for, but then there are carrier proteins, or inhibitors, that allow the expression of certain amounts of color chemicals in certain places. Like your paint tubes, for example. The skin of that tomato has been given certain substances that absorb certain frequencies of light and reflect others, and in proportions determined by genes, akin to your choices of which colors to add to the brew, which colors not to, and how hard to squeeze the tube when you want to add a color. Enough? Can I watch some TV now?"

"Yeah, that's more than I wanted, actually."

"OK, here comes TV." She jumped onto a futon and sighed as she played with the remote control before she turned on the TV. An advertisement was the first thing she saw. It's an advertisement for the EZBlaster©. "Blast away leaves and dirt with its awesome Blasting power!" She turned off the TV and skipped into the bedroom to talk to Angelina.

Angelina tried to persuade the themes of what Mirabelle said into her tomato still life.

Chemical colors, transportation, frequencies, and proportions. She saw a new type of tomato, colors blended over the years by the bravest of butterflies and scents sought after by the newly blossomed chemists. She melted inaccurate preconceptions in her mind: Florentine cafés, tortellini, and meaty men plotting large eating events and vendettas.

"Angelina, have you spoken to Kyle...Angelina? Hello?"

Angelina was deep in concentration. It took her a few moments to come to.

"How can you ask me a question like that right now? I was just about to be able to think about something else."

"Oh...sorry. Well, have you? I wanna know. Come on."

"No. I haven't heard from him."

"The other day, you...mentioned why he's there. What was it again, an old friend of his?"

Silence from Angelina. She casually looked at Mirabelle. "No, it's not a friend of his. Well, it is. I guess it's the very best of his friends, actually. An old girlfriend of his that he can't seem to...to stop loving, I guess. He really seems to like being with me, and he appreciates things in me that I love about myself. But..."

"So why is he there?"

"Because he needs to figure out who he's in love with. If it's me, then I want him to know that, because I'm in love with him. If it's her, and he's just seeing her in me, then I want him to know that too. I don't know what he'll do. I really don't. I mean, either way, I understand, and I want the best for him."

"What about you?"

"What do you mean?"

"I mean, what about yourself. Making yourself happy, you're just gonna let him do the deciding on who wants to be with who."

"No. No. No, not at all. He knows what I want and what Mirabelle does. Do you think he's gonna hurt my feelings if he chooses to spend his life with her?"

Mirabelle stepped away from Angelina and sat on her bed. She felt a little dizzy. She was silent and found it hard to listen to Angelina. She was single after all, and the thought of being in love with someone and letting them go was so strange to her.

"I know what he's going through. I know all too well what it's like to not know if you're in love with someone or not. I mean, come on, that's the whole story behind painting for me.

One minute I'm attached forever to a brush stroke, and then I want to trash it hard."

Angelina started in again.

"But seriously, he resembles something I really want. He resembles someone I could really love. I've been in love with men. I've been in love and haven't been able to decide if I'm in love, and then I've been in love and haven't been able to decide how many people I'm in love with. I guess the only thing I know these days is that I'm not into polygamy. I'm not interested in more than one lover. Mirabelle? Am I talking to you or to the tomatoes?"

After the two broad strokes of a deep red cut during this conversation, Angelina turned her canvas to Mirabelle, who has by now stopped listening to Angelina and is pondering her own misery and loneliness.

Mirabelle sauntered over and pointed to the large red blotches on the canvas.

"The tomatoes," she says.

CHAPTER 28

The sharp sun was a few degrees above the horizon. It pierced even his squinted eyes. He walked in short angular lines, constantly changing direction, like a bat in humid summer. He stumbled. He kicked some sand into someone's face. They vaguely tried to provoke him into feeling guilty for it, but gave up after he passed.

His face achieved a crimson worthy of Mr. Stanzel's extended index finger. At the apex of my redness, Kyle runs into Meghan.

He was totally humiliated when she looked at me. She chose to humiliate me even further. She began to get dressed. She put on her sandals first and threatened to create even more distance between them.

She did not seem surprised to see him. She avoided speaking in any way that would indicate a surprise, something new, or the unexpected. Once she had her things gathered in her arms, she stood still and started to talk to me.

"You know what…I came here to think about you. I came here to think about us. Us together. But only to think. I didn't want to conjure you. I didn't want us to actually be together."

She put a lot of emphasis on "be." Her voice climbed and climbed as she spoke to Blythe.

"If I wanted you to be here, I would have asked you to be here. If…since…well…what the hell are you doing here? I am here to figure things out for myself. For myself implies by myself. For myself, by myself, or anything synonymous, homologous, or anything even close to isolation, selfdom, non-otherness does…not…mean…" she says with a didactic pause in between each word. She stops, utters guttural frustration, and then quietly finishes: "with you."

She radiated heat and rash at him; he almost had to shield his eyes more than from the Sun, and he thought she was the most beautiful person, in both form and content, in her outward appearance of peaceful beach-going and her inner passion and anger. Her red chest heaved with her last sentence. She caught her breath. She huffed a few times. Pure anger huffing, not even emotional. Her sun-blonded, briny hair shone in the red sun and gold-white beach sand. He saw one hair leave her head and fall into the sand. It gathered his attention all at once, and he almost bent down to pick it up. For the first time in a long time, Kyle felt loved, and he realized that she was still in love with him.

He wanted her to grab him and squeeze tight and feel like it is making her happy. Then he wanted her to release when she could tell he'd had enough and kiss him long and hard with reckless abandon for beach propriety or privacy. And kiss him long enough to get him to come back to her hotel room, and they do not make love, just hold each other long enough to fall asleep in the warm air. We shift every now and then and hold our sunburned bodies closer to each other.

But that is called dreaming. And what really happened is she walked away rather abruptly. And had this been in a later part of life, sure, Kyle would have gotten up and had enough conviction to make her realize that she was the only person in the world who was going to make him happy. She was the only one who had enough personality, enough anger, and enough joy in her eyes to make him stay in love.

And so he sat down in the sand. He sat down on top of her footprints and raked his hands through the hot sand. The sweat on his legs and arms trapped sand and flat sticky seashells. Grain after grain passed through hot skin, and he tried to look at each one. He tried to look for her hair in the sand. He passed it through his hand for what seemed like hours, taking a scoop from a different place on the beach every time and putting it back where it came from. After one perfectly beautiful sand cascade, which convinced him that he was coming down with some sort of obsessional disorder or something, he walked to his car and started driving back to Paris alone.

CHAPTER 29

Decimation

The destiny of a piece of rock lies in its eventual decimation. The destiny of a piece of wood under the kinetic friction of a bunch of pieces of sand is to become, in one sense, decimated, but in another, refined from sharp into something smooth. This is the phenomenon of sanding that Angelina tries to capture in her post-tomato art. She coated the apartment floor in sand and fine woodchips like hamster bedding and uses the daily input of her feet—the morning rise, afternoon scramble, and evening energy bursts—to mix the two components into various stages of material. In hallways, wispy sand yields to the directional confines of the space it lies in, and guileful woodchips, lined up alongside the walls, have evaded the crushing foot by dint of the unflagging tendency of a walking person to create an indoor breeze. In the bathroom, a wet slurry of clumped sand seems neatly segregated from the bloated chunks of isolated white meat. In the kitchen, the most equal material has been obtained, a flat dry boardwalk of finely grated wood on scrap pieces of scratched linoleum she laid over the regular linoleum. Let's face it: she hasn't totally abandoned her sense of materials. She realizes that clean, shiny linoleum is something so pure and essential to the human race that she considers living on anything but that to be a sheer waste of enjoyment and an unnatural act of self-torture.

Her feet are clean and soft from the materials on the floor. She ponders the different levels of sanding going on as she walks around the apartment—whether on the ritual walks where she is truly working on the art piece or whether she is just going about her life, though in recent days the distinction between the two is less and less clear—from the sand sanding the floor, to the sand sanding the bottom of her feet, to the sand sanding the wood, to the sand sanding itself into smaller sands, to her feet sanding the floor, and the woodchips sanding her feet, and her feet, with grains of sand embedded in the bottoms of them, sanding the woodchips and the floor and the other sand as well. Although not quite all equal and opposite in her mind. What the wood bears as physical distortion, the sand primarily suffers from increased heat. The ultimate argument for this, she always reminds herself, is the act of using sandpaper. The wood gives way, but the sand does not seem to be changed as much in any characteristic except in its temperature.

There are certain sayings that need to be evoked from time to time, and certain words that convey these sayings more efficiently than others. It will suffice to say: too much time is being spent here on sanding. This is not the real subject of this chapter.

The real subject of this chapter is how Angelina is holding up as she waits for Kyle to come back from Paris. Paris, she's etched it in the sand so many times. Sometimes misspells it to see what she can get: "Pairs", "Parsi", "Sirap", "Apris", "Prisa", "Spria", and others. It's a slight comfort to destroy the world. None of its alternate forms carries the significance of "Paris." "Pairs" comes insultingly close. It is insulting because she is concerned that she and Kyle are not much of a pair. To share her life with herself and her art, that's what she dreads most.

She sits on the sand-free couch, her feet stinging as she picks them up to brush off the sand, sawdust, and woodchips. She rotates and breathes in deeply as she lies down, just as three loud knocks announce a visitor. She knows not to get up. Mirabelle always knocks three times before she walks in the door, which is usually unlocked.

"Hey Angelina. Oh no, you look like someone came in and stole your happy pills. Is everything alright?"

Angelina turns her back towards Mirabelle. She knows she won't take it personally. Mirabelle comes over to relax in her presence; she doesn't need her to pay a lot of attention and participate in stupid conversations to be able to hang out.

"I…uh…slept with a guy named Geronimo last night. Yeah, that was it, Geronimo. He was a big guy, red leather boot and all."

She waits until it finally crosses Angelina's frame of consciousness and then clears her throat.

"Did you hear me?"

"No, what did you say?"

"I said I slept with a guy named Geronimo last night. He was tall, handsome, and he wore those turquoise beads in his hair that a lot of Native Americans wear. Apache or something like that. Apache, Wantabe, you know. He said that he thought I had healing qualities about me. And I got so excited. Me, healer, Western medicine, and tribal medicine united in one being! And then we did this sex ritual thing. It was very kinky."

She finally catches her attention with the sex ritual. Angelina snaps out of her previous mood. She looks over Mirabelle's head to toe, takes in her essence a moment, and then intones, "Geronimo?"

"Yeah, Geronimo." Mirabelle puts on a tight smile and picks at her nails. "What, you don't believe me?"

"Geronimo?!"

"Alright, fine, so I didn't sleep with anyone last night. I studied the cranial nerves."

"Cranial nerves?"

"Ange, are you listening to me, or are you just going to keep repeating everything I say in the interrogative form?"

"Interrogative?"

"Ang…stop it…"

"Alright, chill out, I'm just kidding."

"From cranial nerves?"

"No, from interrogative. Listen, I'm just a little distracted right now. I know you're trying to talk to me and everything.

CHAPTER 30

Lola and Grandpa

In Paris, Blythe passed out in the other room. Spread before Lola, the contents of her suitcase. Old, green, rock-hard plastic, her grandmother's romantic idea of a good birthday present: a hand-me-down suitcase. Storage compartments where vast quantities of underpants and socks have made their way across continents. Side pockets for books of antiquity. Safety straps for documents, ledgers, and mind-numbing information of all sorts.

She had to stow it away, therefore, out of Blythe's way, for it would have been destructive to his sense of self. To preview his past and future in all its details, the jobs he will hold, the sights he will gaze at, the countries he will long for, the names he will forget, the tastes he will savor, the sadness he will not comprehend.

Deeds and mortgage agreements, newspaper clippings and magazine articles, the patina of a thousand viewings on all. Oily checks, menus, bills of fare, receipts of gifts and payment, owings, notices, letters of intent, phone bills never paid, change of address forms, and flunky internet addresses. All these items represent the mode of deception. These are the tools of espionage. The meat and potatoes of life drawing. Not manipulation, but bending. No nepotism, no provisions, no deal-making. Just a nudge and a push here and there, and Lola and George had managed to turn and shape the paths of the lives of their loved ones for nearly two decades.

Lola had met George on the outskirts of her family's Montana ranch. *Traveler,* she called it., a dank, dusty space she rented out with an inheritance from her deceased parents. She turned it into a small bar, a hangout really for her friends and fellows.

In walked George one day. He walked in and piqued the attention of everyone immediately. His gray hair was coarse like denim jeans. An untucked plaid shirt, bottomed out by expensive-looking black shoes, betrayed white socks stained rusty blood red. He made for the bar maliciously, as if starved of drink, a famine of beverage, then slowly backed off like a vehicle in reverse; something had stunned him. Indeed, a vixen in a cowgirl hat had entered the room. As she swaggered through the entrance, her brown hair swished side to side, like a carwash for the old guy's eyes, and she ordered a beer at the bar through suggestive puffs on a cigarillo.

The vixen was Lola, of course. Let's not drag this out beyond reason. She sat beside him, and nearly immediately, he got an excited feeling like he was getting attention from a beautiful woman. Poor old guy, he nearly passed out, face red as a tomato. What he no longer had was a wife; what he did have was money and lots of goodwill. Now he had Lola as his friend and partner.

CHAPTER 31

Lola called Kyle's cell phone one day, her words slow and methodical with less joy than before. She also sounded sober. She asked him to bring her to cancer treatment.

A long pause from Kyle, then a sigh, then a oh-fuck realization moment where he realized this did not sound like a highly treatable or curable cancer, at least as judged by the tone of her voice. He was not yet brave enough to ask, but would find out soon just how bad it was. It was bad.

The first day, Lola was high-strung, nervous, with a pitch or two increase in voice and shaky hands. She had a short temper. They stopped for a coffee, and it took a minute too long, and that was a problem. When someone wants a blueberry muffin and there are none, and shouting and yelling ensue, the stress is enormous.

Cancer, as Kyle would learn over the next few months, was and is and will always be the mindfuck of all mindfucks. It eats away at memories at the same time, lighting them up for replays with added dramatic music and added painful nerve fiber function as if some primordial jellyfish had been working on this neural network for millennia, readying the mind for death mode with new features, new memory highlights, and value. Death is a new brain function yet untouched. The human mind can make incredibly detailed plans and judgments when faced with death, he learned this over a number of rides with Lola to the cancer hospital.

The cancer hospital smelled like insidious death being cleaned up constantly. The escalator always seemed to announce a smell, as if it wafted up, maybe emanating from the green, eerie lights which peeked out between the harsh metal grates. The entryway was large, with large capacity intake corridors; cancer is a volume play, in good ways and bad.

Sometimes he walked Lola into a whitewashed room where she would sit, half content, face a bit paler every visit, and leave her alone at times, and sometimes stay with her at her request. The doctor almost always asked if he was approved to hear everything. They were kind to him naturally and appreciated that he was with her.

Lola often asked him to write things down. He had a very good memory and went through the act of writing things down, but did not need to except for one or two drug names that were foreign. He had a habit of storing memories in rooms of his childhood home, which, over time, assists with rote memorization, also helps if the details are emotionally loaded, as they were with Lola – those take up extra special storage bins in his mind.

Lola would often get a sipping straw-sized needle in the arm, it seemed like gallons of bloodletted, analyzed, and reported upon. The reports were dreary, mechanical in nature to read, huge amounts of normal values mixed with laboratory comments about variations in normal people, commentary about detailed oncologic laboratory tests, fluorescent staining, genetic sequencing, reflexive additive tests, clarifications, mutations, deletions, and notations. So much information was overwhelming for Lola. Kyle could sift through it all, pausing occasionally to take a break with her, take a walk, or rub her back, or stop altogether, sometimes with Kyle sleepless for days when she requested this, as he felt that he had to push her deeper into the decisional pathways, as this was her burden, not his. He usually earmarked a page they had not discussed to come back to it. He did not want to blame himself for untouched topics years later. She was young, she was losing a ton of life, and Kyle wanted to be a helpful journey partner, not be dismissive or diminutive of details. He tried to sit with her for hours at a time, not minutes. He tried to let her determine the pace, which was wildly variable. The doctors were extremely thorough, almost to a fault, which made the visits seem overly clinical and less emotional. He was there for her, in the follow-up hours, days, and weeks, the dreaded late-night phone calls where she was so overwhelmed she did not know what to say or do, she sometimes did not want to live another day. He had found ways to remind her of the joys of life, the value of people, the ridiculous beauty of sunsets, and newfound foods and tastes. Sometimes the thought of petting a dog in a field with friends would get her to sleep, sometimes not.

With Lola's illness, there were good days and bad days, more bad than good, but the good were really good and the bad were worse than expected. On good days, Lola was as bright as the sun, high-powered rays of positivity, energy, poetry, analysis, friendship, help, love, in every direction for unlimited distance. On bad days, it was very bad. Because of her descriptive intellect and compassion for herself as much as for others, she could envision prolonged illness. She was no stranger to drugs, and oddly, at this phase of her life, she swore off painkillers or anything that disrupted her consciousness for more than a brief period of time.

The pain she experienced, she said, woke her mind into action. Every hour of prolonged pain was a great reminder to her of the value of her life. Her natural endorphins kicked in, she said, making her pain almost a pleasant experience, for as she would say, "when the pain is gone, I will be gone and will not return." That saddened Kyle, but he did not press her. One time, she accepted a few pain pills, and she became so sleepy and reminiscent of her days of drug use that it tore away at her remaining happiness and time, so she refused to take much medicine at all, other than chemotherapy. Of course, she smoked some high-potency marijuana from time to time, but infrequently.

CHAPTER 32

"I'm a grandfather!" George said.

"And I'm a grandmother!" his wife and thirty-seven-year-old mate said and chuckled.

"We're grandparents!"

He gave her a hug and sat down to avoid one of his spells, which he felt creeping up with all this excitement. His breathing was labored. He took a sideways glance at his wife's hips as he bent over into a kitchen chair. They always stuck around in the kitchen at moments like these. It was in the kitchen that good things happened, and it was in the kitchen that they felt celebratory.

Each day that died, he felt more alive and yet less and less healthy than his best friend and lifelong partner. Age did not touch her like it had him. His cheeks were once florid and round, but lie hard against his face now, much to the chagrin of his emotions.

"I'd better make some cookies," Jane said. Within minutes, butter and sugar rotate about a smooth wooden spoon, blackened around the edges. Flour escaped the sides of the bowl, vanilla, sugar, and baking soda followed along. Chocolate chips, eager in a bag, awaited the melt and the rise.

George stood up ever so carefully, both his hands on the table. He put his arms around Jane and squeezed her affectionately.   He whispered in her ear, "I'd better go start making some toys."

For years, George had receded to the confines of the barn, a mere fifty yards from the house. The house was literally dropped on top of a Western upstate New York hill in 1968 when there was a surplus of pre-manufactured homes. It was a hundred miles from everything. They had to clear away a significant portion of the trees on the front portion of the property to make way for the tin can. He made good use of the oaks that were cut down.

As he tugged at fallen millennia of growth, labored at lumber, and pulled a thousand splinters, he formed new visions of himself. He imagined an underground chamber where he could hold meetings secret from his wife, secret from everyone but the invitees. He foresaw crude maps of plots, plans for contact networks, the horizontal design of it all present in the organization of his materials in the vacuous bat-infested airspace beneath the barn.

For decades, the plans lay flat like the timber floor of the barn, which covered the secret eight-foot excavation. Complexity gathered there in its own inevitable biological growth. Spider webs glistened in the dark corners. Mice reproduced beyond the hunger of their multitudes. Bats clicked their wings on the wood in search of ants, mites, and mosquitoes. And that was it, for years. Fifteen years passed, and his own family grew larger as well.

There were no aspirations of glory, honor, or even appreciation. His motivation was the tick of his heart and the swelling of his chest he felt when the sun rose every morning as he tended to the rhubarb and asparagus in the garden. The sense that he would nurture generations of plants and animals that would, in future lives, remember him not for what he did but for the sheer simplicity of his ideas.

So what did he need space for? Why did he desire the trickery of hidden caverns and silent nooks?

The answer was ideas. Ideas had always been seductive to him. The idea that he could make a bird fly away merely with a look, that he could sculpt a piece of wood out of nothing other than an image in his mind—in essence turn energy into form that could inspire others—and he could do this all with but ideas and idle time spent set in a wooden chair, stiff enough to provide support but soft enough to lure him into lengthy consideration of long thoughts.

If you think about the real ideas you have, they are the easiest ones to remember. Soft thoughts were quickly cleared from the mind, easily purged by the fluid notion that they will never be realized. Hard, long thoughts, however, remain for long periods of time. In such a mind as George's—which is not prone to lie down when thirsty, nor to let dry flowers die in the sun, nor to let his wife die unhappily, nor to cook an uneaten meal—thoughts like this made his eyes excited with anticipation.

CHAPTER 33

Kyle felt drained as he stood up on the beach. He felt like a million seashells all piled into one breathing space: lost, dry, and brittle. As if the ocean waters would surge upon him, willing to tumble him about in a mix of infinite others, reduce him to the sameness of water. Turn him into salt, brine, sandy nothingness. Turn him into foam, to line the edges of the water, to bathe clumpy algae arms, and dilute the blood of the dead.

He walked towards the dunes. His feet scraped the sand. He kicked up a small sandstorm in front of him and to the sides. He pushed onwards, taking a straight line for a path up the dune to minimize my time on the beach. The sun went back to its status as an enemy.

He found his way back to the car and drove away. He headed to Bordeaux, glad to leave the coast. When he hit Bordeaux, he stopped the car in front of a restaurant. He decided to eat and ponder what he should do.

He stepped into a dark wooden space lined with quiet people at tables against the walls. It seemed the younger crowd sat towards the middle of the room. He looked for a booth, an isolated table, to try to recreate something more familiar, the privacy of a restaurant one may know in New York. He was amazed that the French don't have "booths," it's purely an American contrivance. At best, one or two of them exist in Paris, but be sure they are imported. The cool cooking smoke in the room eased his disappointment, and he took a seat in the middle of a group of tables, mostly two-seaters…he sat for a while and pondered the difficulties he had had seating couples at a restaurant, a venue of mass consumption, an efficient feedery, that catered to six or eight-person tables. His stomach grumbled a few times, and he got up to see if he actually entered a sitting parlor instead of a restaurant. The only other evidence he had that the function of this space was nourishment, aside from the word "restaurant" on the outside of the establishment, was the bones and rice on the plates in front of the old man alongside the wall. No waitress, no bar, no scents, no cook wandering about.

He found a stairway that led to a rooftop bar, a scene soundtracked by cars below, loud American conversations, and a plane slightly overhead. It appeared as if they were mostly sunburned tourists who had underestimated the guile of the bartender. There was nothing quite like the out-of-placeness of a drunken tourist to make you feel welcome and hip.

He took a seat in an umbrella's shade at a well-sanded wooden table with a good view of the street and the crowd. He ordered a drink and some food from the waiter and smoked a cigarette in the warm open air. Luckily, it was not just a two-seater table, but a four-seater, and for some reason, the idea of being alone at a larger table pleased him.

Food came, and he ordered a coffee right away. He rested his head on his hand and ate with the other one, occasionally considered sleeping right there after finishing, but for the coffee. Somewhere, someone played guitar, too confident to be enjoyable. Suddenly, he found himself eased into a sullen satisfaction with the scene. He felt a gentle wave of calm come over the roof like before it rains in the first warm weather of a long, cold winter.

Just then, Meghan appeared at the other end of the table.

If it's been a while since something hit you, then this will be a tough few sentences.

When something hits you, something you have been dwelling on subconsciously for a few months or a few years, it was an exciting affair. One feels a sense of completion and that elation of discovery.

What hit Kyle was the fact that all this time he had been seeing advertisements all over Paris, ads for what looked like alcoholics, addicts of all sorts, problem-riddled people who can't quit holding on to some specific habit. Then, perusing his recall of the night, his hand strayed at one point as he entered the club, and he fingered a small drape that hid a few light switches inside the entryway. He lifted the square foot of blue velvet tapestry, soft to the touch, and uncovered a raised metal insignia, silver in color, which looked like this:

He had to stop for a minute, Didier at his back and about to come over to see what he had his hands in. He seemed concerned, so Kyle released the drape and turned to him.

"What is it? You look alarmed?"

"Nothing. I was just checking out the architecture."

No one will ever know why Kyle came up with that.

"Come on, quit stalling. Don't be intimidated, it's just a club."

Didier winked at Blythe. It was a real wink. Not a wink for support, to show mutual understanding. Nor a wink for emphasis or exaggeration. But a wink to show that he was saying one thing and meaning another. It was an inductive wink, and Kyle wanted to know what he was being let in on as soon as possible. He already knew there was something weird about this club, some connection he had to it, something about the "M." from his past that he could not quite place.

The wink. The insignia. The ads are all over Paris. Kyle was onto something. He was a detective all of a sudden. Experience sprang into action. Who had sent that letter long ago? He asked himself so many questions all at once and raised so many possibilities that he had to stop the car.

Just as he was about to finish his meal, thinking about drinking himself into oblivion, Meghan appeared. He almost coughed up some food and felt he looked disgusting compared to her beautiful, suntanned appearance.

"Meghan? I thought you left."

She sat down.

"I simply cannot believe you came here today."

He thought she sounded upset.

"But to be honest, I am glad you did. We need to talk."

Kyle thought this was the real end. She sounded serious, as if this were the breakup talk to a loved one after the initial hard breakup. The "do-not-under-any-circumstances-ever-call-or-speak-to-me-again" speech. The final breakup of a breakup, smashing all hope to smithereens, where particles break down their very entities to subatomic units in the darkness of space, where things cease to exist, and black holes suck up life into an infinite death of constantly repeated death.

But…then she started talking again, just as Kyle said, "Well, what do you want to talk about…"

"We have deep love between us, that much is clear, but we have some issues."

Kyle noticed happy tears forming in her eyes.

"As I was saying… I cannot believe you came here today. I don't even know what to say. As I sat on the beach today, I realized that I came here to clear my head and try to make some decisions. I was going to decide what to do with myself for a year or two. And just about as I was going to make a decision that I did not want to do it alone…well, look who showed up. You Kyle. And you were exactly what I was hoping for."

"I just…it's just love Meghan. I'm not going to stop loving you, and I don't think we should be apart."

She grabbed his hand, and for the first time in a long time, Kyle felt some happiness creep back in.

"Just stop there, Kyle. Nothing you will say will be better than just saying that. I agree. I love you too. I want to find a way to make it work.   Even though we are both prone to needing space and independence, we can try to find a way."

They both now held both hands, and she sat down next to him, and they immediately kissed each other passionately. People stared at them the way people stare at couples who embrace in public.   They could not help themselves.

Meghan said, "You're a real pain in the ass sometimes, and you suffocate me."

Kyle said, "You are rude and mean to me so often, I don't know what to do."

"I don't need you telling me what to do and what not to do."

"If we trust each other and love each other, so many parts of our lives will be so much more enjoyable."

There were long pauses with deep stares in between these comments, and sometimes laughs, and sometimes long, slow kissing.

"Leave me alone sometimes when I need to be left alone."

"Don't be so distant. You can just tell me how you feel, and I won't feel bad about it."

And they went back and forth like this for an hour.

"Drive us to a hotel, I want to stay together now and for a long time."

Kyle drove them, straight and quietly, to a hotel.

They did not say much the rest of the night. The necessary words had been said. The rest of the night was mostly sweaty passionate embraces, gut-wrenching sex, words of love, and wine and champagne ordered to the room in between.

They stayed in the hotel for two days and did not come out for long, other than to get some basic groceries and toiletries not included at the hotel.

For hours at a time, they did not speak, just slept and embraced one another as if they had no need for anything else.

"We can fly home in a few days. I don't want to stay in Paris much longer. I came here to find my independence, and I feel good about that now."

"How much packing do I have to do for you?"

"I did most of it already."

"You were…already packed to go?"

"No, just partially packed, ready for a change."

CHAPTER 34

It doesn't seem like a state. Its borders were fuzzy, ill-defined as crusty lines drawn on maps when viewed under microscopes. The nation-state was less present here. The borders are inviting and seductive. Waves pull back, not forward, suck you into the water as if your dead body, bones, and filth would enrich the ocean and feed its inhabitants. Sea scythe rocks slit skin quite easily, and it hurts because of the salt. Its borders were porous, easily sailed or swum. The essential pull of the ocean was mystifying. Exfoliation upon the concentric rock, dead calcified beings pretend to eat skin. The coral is an ineffable effigy of nature, the world full of mystic fatness, unearthly round and confusing as hell.

Lola liked the beach sand here and, therefore, chose Honolulu as the place where she would settle down for some undetermined period of time to die. She knew it was coming. She couldn't give up the alcohol and the drugs, and the wonderful Doctor Pardon, despite his unending kindness and good looks, had informed her she was no longer a transplant candidate. Anyways, there was a shortage of livers for her anyway. She was fucked, so she was going to live somewhere beautiful that limited her lifestyle as little as possible. The only problem was that she was far from everything here. She used the 12-hour flights as time to arrange her thoughts.

About three months into her Hawaii vacation, she fell ill. Her eyeballs turned into yellow ping pong balls, and she was as confused as a psychotic person. She actually didn't mind the feeling, but she ended up lost in her own neighborhood and got brought to the hospital by three stoned surfers whose surfboard she tried to sleep on. They were kind souls and had apparently seen cirrhotic like this before, as in their alcoholic fathers, and knew what she needed.

In the emergency room, she was yellow as a school bus, confused, and angry.

"Give me so much goddamn syrup that I shit my fucking brains out."

"I want to…I want to be shitting the fucking Nile River."

"I want people riding my shit in fucking river rafts."

"I want rapids of shit. Diarrhea fucking Niagara Falls. Niagara Falls out of my ass."

"I want to cure fucking droughts with my diarrhea."

"I want to shit my brains out now, right so…please give me that damn syrup…I have things to do…please…now."

These were the kinds of things she was yelling at the ER staff. And they put her in the ICU because her lungs filled up with fluid.

"You shouldn't have been drinking alcohol and smoking marijuana, Ms. Lola. We will do what we can for you, but at this time, with the ongoing drinking, we cannot send you to a liver transplant program."

"That wasn't drinking, sweetheart, that was just living. I ain't an alcoholic big Kahuna, okay?"

With that, she desaturated to 85% and was placed on a ventilator.

CHAPTER 35

The Death Unit

Lola's chest went quietly up and down slightly in quiet bellows motion. The insane beeps were constant and a constant reminder of every precious heartbeat. Lola lay in a sedated daze, her arms and legs numb, her mind calmly singing to the pathetic, calming death music the nurses believed helped sick people ease into one final long goodnight. But Lola protested their existence with each sad B flat. She was not going to die, at least not while it was under her control.

The nurse whispered soft, lovely words into her ear as she wiped her rear end softly. "No wounds. Good skin. You look at healthy Lola, I think you really have a shot here. You can pull through."

But Lola recalled, despite the fentanyl haze, that doctors had prognosticated weeks or less. That was months ago. Lola had been in the intensive care unit with an abdominal infection and some transient hemodialysis. She had been putting off the liver biopsy for several years. She wanted a needle in her liver less than she wanted a sharp Japanese blade penetrated inside her skull from temple to temple.

In desperation, apparently, she had provided half consent to a liver biopsy a few days ago – she barely recalled.

Just then, the medical resident on the unit came into the room. He seemed frantic. Lola thought she was going to die. The nurse and the resident chatted hurriedly, as if something of great urgency was happening.

Lola's breathing tube had just been removed, and with it, a few days of procrastinated phlegm and goop had been birthed out of her airways. Lola was coughing and sickly, but alive and awake.

"Lola," he said, "Hey there, I'm the chief medical fellow on the gastroenterology unit. My name is Marshall. I've just got back the results of your liver biopsy."

Lola had just been extubated, and with half-drunk eyes but a wide awake mind, she nodded yes and hello.

"I need some damn coffee. Badly."

Marshall smiled and said, "We will get you some coffee soon," in typical dismissive doctor style. As in, we don't care about your desires; we care about your life.

"I have some good news. Your liver is not as bad as we thought. You appear to have what we call autoimmune hepatitis. It's hugely inflamed; however, we think we can save your liver with the right combo of medications. There will be side effects to immunosuppressants, but we think you will live a long life. You have not yet had full treatment. Potentially, you can live long enough to get a liver transplant and live a full life. Also, more good news, you do not have any viral hepatitis, which improves the chances of transplant success, and the safety of medical treatment for your inflamed liver."

"But Dr. Pardon said my liver was shot. And I'm in critical condition in the death unit."

"We know that Lola, we spoke with your doctor this morning. He expressed his desire to say not only hello, but to wish you the best. He also said to yell at you about all your marijuana smoking and your persistent refusal to get a liver biopsy. He said he had been asking you for years."

"Damn, Pardon, he has such a good memory. Can't he just forget some things I say and do?"

Marshall chuckled and smiled.

"We and he are doing our jobs, Lola. We want to get started on treatment right away, like today, Lola. We think you are going to improve rapidly."

"Improve? What do you mean by " improve? I'm looking at certain death with liver failure."

"Your liver has improved markedly under our care, Lola. We tuned you up over the last few days. With pulse dose steroids, your liver is headed in the right direction, and we will start more powerful medications today if you agree to reduce inflammation. We think the prognosis is quite good."

Lola was, for one of the first times in her expressive artistic life, a bit at a loss for words. Marshall was the kindest doctor she had ever met, second to Dr. Pardon, of course.

"You mean I'm not going to die soon?"

"We don't think so."

"Well then, get me fucking cup of coffee and get me out of this hellhole, I've got a lot of things to do," said Lola, emphatically and quite seriously.

Marshall smiled and seemed to well up a bit. He seemed very confident in his prognosis.

She started crying like she had been waiting to cry for herself and for her own mortality, harder than she had ever cried before.

She did that for a little while. She also thought deeply about all the other tragedies she had heard about in her brief time in the ICU. She recalled several folks, in the back of her mind, that she had absorbed through snippets of nurse and doctor conversations, who were brought in in critical condition, and perished hours later. She knew of a young man down the hallway with a heart attack who kept dying, and the family was overcome. There were three elderly people dying from pneumonia on the unit, and a young person with brain edema who was likely brain dead.

She felt so lucky. She was close to exiting the death unit.

Then she stopped feeling sorry for herself and started thinking about the future.

CHAPTER 36

Kyle had become nosy and overconfident, poking around Lola's apartment.

He was there to check on her. He had been in Paris when she was hospitalized. He had not known she had been close to death. No one had. Once again, Lola had suffered through her life mostly alone. Kyle told her how sad he felt for her and how hard it must be.

She changed some bandages on some healing wounds, which were almost totally resolved.

"Well, scientist, you see I'm not totally alone."

Kyle fumbled into some drawers, looking for old pictures or joints.

He found a few sheets of familiar paper in the center drawer, hidden under some medical pamphlets. He fingered them, oddly familiar.

"I've actually had someone with me for a long time. His name is D…"

Kyle interrupted her.

"Sorry, Lola, oh, Lola, can I ask you something?"

"Yes, Kyle, what is it?"

Kyle was quiet for a moment, but finally said straight to Lola.

"Where did you get this paper?"

CHAPTER 37

Kyle and Meghan settled into a 4th-floor walk-up in New York. Life was good. They were happy to be together, worked out their differences over many a Chinese food restaurant, slowly touring practically all of them in this hungry late-night city. They ate their way broke, loved each other like crazy, and had the time of their lives.

One day, Kyle got a call from his mother. She said that Grandpa George had died. Kyle was sad but was still riding the high of getting back with Meghan, so it did not hit like a death blow, more like a celebration of life.

The family mourned George for a few weeks, then had a family get-together at Lake Chautauqua.

A package came in the mail from a courier toward the end of the trip, and a driver in a white van walked up and hand-delivered a musty package directly to Kyle after asking the other family members who was named Kyle.

"Are you Kyle Blythe?"

"I am."

"My name is Michael Anderson. I run a shipping company. I was paid a good amount of money to hand this to you a long time ago. I have been sitting on this a long ass time."

It was addressed "To: Kyle Blythe," and the courier said it had been delivered by a company that left no address and no return phone number. The shipment had been scheduled 10-15 years ago, he said, paid in cash by someone who fit George's description. Kyle scratched his head and was not truly surprised to find a stylized M. on the package return label section, no address, no other information.

"Thank you."

The man walked away abruptly.

Kyle stared at the package, then tore it open.

Inside were only two items:

A map of George's property with a big X marked deep in the largest field of the property, and a brief letter to Kyle.

For your eyes only, mark the letter. There were instructions to never share with anyone, not spouse, family, or lawyer.

"Dear Kyle-

By now, you should know that I've been up to some nonsense for a few years. I saved a man's life about 30 years ago while traveling abroad. His name was G. I will not share more details. He had become an alcoholic, was living on the streets of New York City, and was close to death when I found him. I tripped over him while walking out of a bar. I got him a hotel room for two weeks, detoxed him, and got to know him a bit. Turns out he was a billionaire who had lost his wife, the founder of an internet company that had sold for a few billion dollars.

G. and I started a company to help people. We call it M. This is the source of all the logos you've been finding popping up all over the place.

All you have to do is find the suitcase I've buried in the family farm by the enclosed map. X marks the spot! If you want, carry on the tradition. Help people. You should now know how we do it, as we've been helping you for a few years. Just go with your heart, and you'll find you're not alone; there are many others to help you keep the tradition. The foundation is rich and deeply established in most countries. All you have to do is connect with M. and they will help you get started. They've been given your name and put you in charge if you accept the duty. There is plenty of money to support yourself, not richly, Kyle, just enough.

And most of all, Kyle, have fun, and do it with someone you love, and then pass it on to anyone you trust!

Love,

Grandpa

P.S. Don't tell a soul other than people you trust 100% because they will want the funds, and we only give the funds to people who need it most."

Blythe did not show it to anyone. He crumpled the letter in his pocket and later burned it. He wanted to tell Meghan so badly, and one day he would, but not right away.

Kyle returned to the celebration and made up a story that it was a routine legal matter related to the will. He had shared grandpa's will with the family a couple of days later, and for all the family knew, the matter was closed.

He had a hard time sleeping that night. He set an alarm for 5 AM before everyone else would be up and headed out to the rear of the main farm field, well out of sight. It was barely light.

He sounded the spot marked X on the map indicated by a small group of six-inch boulders lying in a small line of 3 next to a tree. The X on the map indicated the 3rd boulder away from the tree was the place to dig.

He moved the 3rd boulder and started digging.

At the bottom of a six-inch hole, Blythe finally hit something. It felt plastic and hollow. Eventually, it turned green, and flat, dirty plastic emerged as he scraped away the last traces of dirt and dug around the edges of something the size of a suitcase. It was a suitcase for crying out loud. A big ugly sixties-green suitcase, hard plastic. He grabbed it by the handle and yanked it out of the dirt, which made a soft sucking sound in the moist dirt below.

He laid the case on the ground outside the hole, his hands shaky and tired and forearms burly and sweaty. He took off his gray flannel shirt and used it to wipe away the dirt on top. Much to his astonishment, what became clear all of a sudden, as he fingered for the final time a piece of metal screwed onto the top of the case in the shape of the now familiar "M" came into view. Blythe fiddled with the five-digit lock beneath the handle, and laughed to himself since he already knew the combination – the one his grandpa had always used…1,2,3,4,5.   He laughed out loud and entered the combination. The lock snapped open, and he swung open the case.

Inside: a piece of paper and a key. The paper read, in grandpa's familiar, simple handwriting:

"You're it. Have fun with this. Love, Grandpa."

The key was small, well-worn, and absent any label or writing. He had only one thought. He remembered grandpa used to keep a safe-deposit box at a local bank.

Blythe sat next to the case in the dirt, held the key and paper in his hand, and started laughing out loud to himself. He was smiling, but sort of crying at the same time. He thought of Meghan and how he wished she were here next to him. Over time, he would bring her into this, but not right away, until he figured it all out.

Eventually, he stood up, grabbed the suitcase, and carried it to the road, where he started walking into town to grab some breakfast and head to the local bank when it opened.